CLUSTER

BY

RENEE MILLER

Copyright © 2022 by Renee Miller

All Rights Reserved.

No part of this book may be reproduced, distributed or transmitted in any form or by any means without the author's written consent, except for the purposes of review

Cover Design © 2021 by Don Noble

https://roosterrepublicpress.com

ISBN-13: 978-1-947522-49-7

This book is a work of fiction. Names, characters, places and incidents are either a product of the author's fertile imagination or are used fictitiously. Any resemblance to actual events, places or persons, living or dead, is entirely coincidental.

READ UNTIL YOU BLEED!

CHAPTER 1

BAKER PLANTATION, 1848

Elizabeth lay for hours watching prisms of light expand and distort the shapes and colors surrounding her. The pain in her eyes expanded with them, wrapping around her head, reaching downward until it brushed the back of her neck.

Somewhere beyond her bedroom door, John cried. He always cried. Morning, noon and night. The nurse was supposed to keep him quiet. She told her at least a dozen times that day. Now his cries became hysterical, punctuated by distinct shrieks and hiccups. The nurse must have gone to bed.

"Lazy cow," Elizabeth mumbled as she forced herself from the bed. Slowly, stumbling as the pain in her head intensified, she managed to walk to the door and then into the hallway.

"Mama?" Rebecca's voice appeared so suddenly that Elizabeth jumped. "My head hurts."

Elizabeth turned. Rebecca leaned against the wall, stuffed rabbit clutched to her chest.

She'd fooled herself into believing the children might be spared. Rebecca's bloodshot eyes and paper white cheeks put an end to that delusion.

As she tried to form the words to tell her daughter it'd

be okay, the pain in Elizabeth's head dug deep. It stole her voice, her breath, her ability to form a thought and hold onto it.

She pressed the top of her nose and breathed deeply and slowly. One by one, the pain took them. The field hands first, and then her husband, William. Elizabeth's maid came next, probably the direct result of her sharing William's bed every third day, and then the kitchen staff. Two days ago, Elizabeth fell ill. Now, the children suffered. It would not stop. The doctor assured her it wasn't lethal, but how long could they go on like this? If the affliction couldn't even be treated, could it be cured? Would this state of constant pain and suffering be her life forever?

What kind of mother allowed her children to endure such torment? Something had to be done.

William suggested it wasn't illness at all. He said the fires of hell burned in his skull, which could only mean one thing; the Devil had gotten inside of them. They'd sought council from Reverend James. He tried to help, but the evil would not be cast out. William refused to continue suffering. His attempt to kill himself and the devil was thwarted, though, by a couple of well-meaning stable boys.

"I want to sleep, but my head hurts too much," Rebecca said. "I'm so tired, Mama."

Sleep. Yes. Elizabeth turned the word around in her overheated brain. It felt good. Right. Only rest could save them. A lot of it.

She smiled. "It's okay, sweetheart. Mama will help you."

"But John's crying. You should go to him."

"I'll see to him first. Go to bed and wait for me. Soon, we'll all sleep."

* * *

"The exorcism didn't work," Reverend James said. "I've tried everything, but we're up against something powerful.

Their headaches continue and the death toll rises every day. Three housemaids were found hanging in the barn this morning. The boy that works with the horses says they did it themselves, but they were God fearing women. I can't see them taking their own lives. They would never commit such a mortal sin."

"You think it was the boy?" Charles asked. "Perhaps he's ill and went mad like the others."

"No. He is well. I examined him myself this morning. Stays away from the main house, so he's avoided contact with the afflicted, but he cut the maids down and laid them out before calling for the foreman. It's likely he's infected now or will be soon."

Charles said a prayer for the women and the boy. And then he prayed that whatever had infected them stayed on the Bakers' land. Selfish, yes, but surely an entire household would be enough to satisfy whatever demons tormented them. Could demons travel? Would they move more than ten miles for just a couple of souls? He eyed James. The man had spent hours at the Bakers' and now he stood in Charles' kitchen, potentially spreading the illness.

He took a step backward. "If the demon is passed so easily, you shouldn't minister to them anymore. It's too dangerous."

"God protects me. I am not afraid."

He wished he shared James's unwavering faith in the Lord. As of late, Charles found himself doubting God's plan increasingly, wondering if He had abandoned them entirely.

Just yesterday, Charles woke with a powerful throbbing in his head, and feared the worst. It abated, though. He saw no reason to worry his wife or James over it. Probably just his body reacting to the stress of what was happening to his neighbors or his imagination tormenting him with the thing he currently feared most. A mind over matter thing, as his mother liked to say.

"And William's taken to roaming the house without a

stitch of clothing," James continued. "Says the fabric tears his skin."

"Very unlike William."

"Indeed. As was his attempt on his life. He's a God-fearing man and would never commit such a sin if he were in his right mind."

"Good thing those lads found him before it was too late."

"Maybe if they hadn't, Elizabeth wouldn't be ill."

Charles shook his head.

"For three nights, she wailed from the balcony of her bedroom, begging for God to take her or her babies, while scratching at her own flesh," James said. "We convinced her to come inside and rest. I thought she had settled, but last night, she attempted to smother the infant. Thankfully, the child's nurse stopped her."

"I can't imagine Elizabeth harming her children. They're her life."

"The demon inside is controlling her. We've tried tying her down to her bed, but she gets free every time."

"What are we to do?" Charles asked.

"Pray. It's all we can do."

"Could it be illness, as Doc believes? Maybe they suffer from some kind of brain infection that requires medication rather than prayer. I heard such infections can cause madness."

"No," Reverend James closed his bible. "It comes and goes. Strikes one and not another, and it turns folks into a shadow of their former selves. Sometimes, it makes them monstrous."

"I have heard of fevers causing the same symptoms."

"Yes, but illness is constant. It's predictable and it reacts to treatment. I've never seen anything like this. Those lights..."

"Were a miracle from God, you said."

"And I believed that to be true." A tear slipped down his cheek. "I fear the Devil may have fooled me, Charles. Fooled all of us."

Charles jumped at the sound of a knock on the door. James's sister, Mary, entered. Her face was pale. Cheeks wet with tears.

"Oh, James," she said. "It's gotten worse."

"What is it?"

"She's killed them."

"Killed who?"

"The children."

Charles swallowed the bile that stung his throat. The throbbing in his head returned, but he was careful not to touch the source of the pain. "Who has killed the children?"

"Elizabeth. She's smothered all of them. Even the babe. The girl watching over her fell asleep and she... I can't bear to speak of what I saw."

James cursed. The profanity was so sudden, so unlike him, that it scared Charles more than the thought of a mother so out of touch with reality, she'd harm her own children.

"Where is William?" James asked.

Mary wiped her eyes. "They've locked both him and Elizabeth in the cellar. He tried to cut his own eyes out with a butter knife, but the cook found him and put a stop to it. He's bound so he cannot harm himself further."

"We have to help them," Charles said. "Find a city doctor to treat them, perhaps." If a doctor could cure them, then the pain in Charles's head might not mean what he feared it would.

"They don't need a physician," James said. "They need God."

"Well, you said the bishop was due here next month. We could send word. Beg him to come now."

James sighed. "I'm afraid there isn't time. We must deal with this ourselves, before it spreads."

"What are you saying?"

"There is but one way to purge the evil trapped inside that house and those fields."

6 CLUSTER

Charles knew what he was about to say. They couldn't. Wouldn't. Maybe he was wrong. "How?"

"Send the demons back to Hell."

"God have mercy on us." And himself. He prayed silently that the sparks igniting in his brain weren't the same sparks causing William and Elizabeth to go mad.

"They require His mercy, Charles, and it's up to us to deliver it. We are out of options."

"Just the sick ones. I'll get some men together. We'll clear the healthy from the plantation first."

"No," James stared at the worn leather cover of his bible. "The Devil is cunning. He will hide when he realizes what we're doing. The only way to eliminate his presence is to burn them all."

* * *

"We don't have to do this," Constance said.

"Reverend says it's the only way. Do you think I want to be part of this? There are children in that house."

"They're human beings, Charles. We can't just...."

"James says it's the only way to purge the demons."

"Even a man of God doesn't know everything. This is sinful. How do we know the devil isn't in James as well? He could be putting these ideas in his head and forcing him to murder those poor souls."

"James is fine." Charles laced his boots, but he didn't look at her as he spoke. "Ever since those lights burned up William's corn field, that whole place hasn't been right. You know that."

"And the crops flourished," she argued. They'd all agreed those lights were sent from Heaven. A sign from God that the hard times were over. "We can't burn them without knowing for sure it's the Devil and not illness."

Charles stood. He pulled on his jacket, and then picked up the can of petrol he'd retrieved from the barn. "Whatever is in those folks is evil. Do you want it to spread here? Want to lose your mind one day and kill your children like Elizabeth did?"

She shook her head. "I don't, but they're sick Charles. What they need is a doctor, not a death sentence."

"Doc's been there time and again, and now he reckons he's got the madness too. Hasn't had a day in two weeks without pain in his head. Even he, being a man of science, agrees with us. Went into the house on his own. Just wants the evil in his brain to be silenced."

"It's just so cruel."

"What's cruel is to allow those people to continue suffering. We're showing them mercy."

"They should be isolated, so the sickness can run its course. The strong will survive. We are not murderers."

"I'm done talking about it. Decision's been made. You stay here with the kids and you don't have to murder anyone. I'll be home once it's done."

CHAPTER 2

PRESENT DAY

Jerry stepped on the skull before he saw it. The slight percussion it made under his feet as it shattered made him look down. When he what he'd done, his heart skipped a few beats.

"Hold on!" he yelled to Bill, who swung the backhoe toward the hole. "I just... fuck. There's a body in here."

"What?"

"We just dug up a body."

"No kidding. Hang on. I wanna see." Bill climbed down from the backhoe and ran around the perimeter of the hole.

Now they'd have to call the cops. Work would have to stop until they figured out what a human skull was doing in the ground. The lot had been abandoned for a couple of decades at least. Before that, Jerry's grandfather had told him that an old plantation house occupied the spot, which had been converted into a triplex, and then left to rot until the city condemned it and tore it down.

Jerry knelt, brushed the dirt away from the skull, and revealed a second one in the process. "Jesus, fuck my mother. Damn it! I have the worst fucking luck. Swear to God."

"Why? Just have to dig them up and we can keep going."

"No," Jerry rubbed his eyes. "They'll want to identify them and look for more. That alone could take weeks."

"Does it smell?" Bill stood at the edge of what would eventually be the foundation of the new mall.

"Nah, it's just bones. Been here a while."

"Shit."

"Yeah," Jerry said. "Bring me a shovel."

Bill disappeared for several seconds, returning with two shovels. He tossed one down to Jerry and then jumped down to join him. "Shouldn't we call the cops? Don't want to mess up a crime scene or anything."

"I just want to clear some of this dirt away. See what we've got. If this is like an Indian burial spot or whatever, we're screwed. They'll pull our permits. It'll be a cluster-fuck of court bullshit and bleeding hearts protesting the build. Head office is going to freak out."

"Could just get rid of them. Pretend like we never found them."

"If anyone finds out, we'd get jail time. No job is worth that."

"Why? Not like we killed them."

"We'd just get in shit, okay. We have to do the right thing."

They gently scraped away the soil with the tips of their shovels. As they did so, Jerry's heart sank. More bones. Not just skulls. Dozens of legs, ribs, skulls, arms and pieces of moldy fabric lined the entire left side of the hole.

"Wow," Bill said. "That's a lot of bodies."

Jerry knelt. He picked up a small, baseball sized skull, and turned it around. "This looks like a baby's skull."

"Don't touch it. Cops will be all up in your shit if you ruin the evidence."

"It's been here a long time. I doubt they'll get any prints off them. I'll just say I fell and touched it by mistake."

"I seen a lot of weird things in the ground, but this is some creepy ass shit."

"I'll call Matt at head office," Jerry said as he tossed the skull onto the ground. "And then I'll let him call the cops."

"Should I send everyone home?"

"Just tell them to take a long lunch. Maybe it won't be so bad and we'll be able to work around it."

* * *

Six hours after arriving at the site, Al was ready to dig. Because the sun had set by that time, they had to wait another hour for the floodlights to be set up. Clive was used to his boss's annoying tendency to over analyze every situation, but it still bugged him that every single job moved at a snail's pace. They could achieve so much more, maybe even solve more cases, if he'd just do his job instead of fretting over every single detail.

Eventually, Clive returned to the van. Standing around with his thumb up his ass while someone else got to do the fun stuff was boring. Now he sat on the bumper, drinking bottled water and snacking on the slightly stale Doritos he found in Al's glovebox.

"Hey, Clive?" Al called. "Can you bring me more bags?"

Clive finished his water and then grabbed a box of evidence bags from the back of the van. He walked the short distance to where his boss lay on his belly, carefully brushing soil away from the bones.

He passed the bags down. Al opened one, put a bit of cloth inside and then sealed it. "I'll need you to tag all of these," he pointed to the stack of bags beside him. "Makes sure to include the part of the grid they came from."

"Okay. All of it is from this section?"

"Yes. Not sure if they're all relevant, some of it could be just garbage collected in the ground over the years, but better to take it all."

Clive knelt, scooped up the bags containing assorted items, some cloth-like materials, while others appeared to be bits of glass and pottery, and then stood. "Think it's Aboriginal?"

"No. Most of these are Caucasian, although there are two skulls over there that might be African American, and the little one here," he pointed to a half-buried skull about two thirds the size of the others, "is Asian, I think. We'll have to get Rita to look at it more closely, but I'm almost positive."

"It's amazing how you can know that shit just by looking at them."

"Spent many years believing I'd be an archaeologist," Al said. "Who knew fucking around with Daddy's money would be useful when I decided to go into forensics, eh?"

The wind picked up, stirring the loose dirt around. Clive covered his face, but still got a mouthful of it. Al must've got a lungful. He coughed, spit and then cursed.

"Get me some water?" he said between gags and sputters.

Clive stood. He couldn't wait for the day when he wasn't the team's gopher anymore. Just another month. Once he passed the exams, he'd be a full-on investigator. No more of this intern crap. Although Al would probably make him fetch shit until he died.

He grabbed a bottle from the case someone had set on a table set up near the excavation site, and then tossed it to Al. Al stood as well, twisted off the cap and then drank half of it in what seemed like a single gulp. He put the lid back on and tossed it back to Clive.

"This is a big site," Al said. "So, we're going to need a full team. It'll take me days to do this on my own."

"I can help."

Al shook his head. "Call the office. I'm going to need experts. Sorry, Clive, but you're still a baby, and while this is an enjoyable experience, you don't know enough to be any help."

"You could use the opportunity to teach me what I don't know," Clive thought, but didn't say the words aloud.

"Some of these remains show signs of trauma," Al continued. "While others appear to have died naturally. Not sure if it's an old graveyard or the dumping grounds of a serial killer. Could be both."

"How long do you think they've been buried here?"

"Decades."

"If it's a graveyard, wouldn't there be coffins?"

"Not necessarily. If this is an old family plot, they might have just wrapped the bodies and buried them."

"A family of multiple ethnicities?" Clive asked.

"Slaves."

"Oh."

"This piece of land was in the Baker family for at least a hundred years. I think it was a plantation at some point. That means, there were probably slaves. It's a sad part of our history, but it happened just the same."

"No, I meant..." Clive took a breath. "Isn't it unusual to bury slaves with the family, though?"

"Yes."

"So..." he stared at the massive depression in the ground. "How many people should I say you need to work this thing?"

"As many as they can spare. Get this done as quickly as we can. Got a storm moving in. It'll be a shit show if we can't get most of it excavated before the rain. Might as well tell them to bring some tents too, just in case."

Clive walked away as he dialed dispatch on his phone. His throat was so dry it stung, so he opened the water bottle and finished what Al left behind.

"Hey, Clive," Jessica answered. "What's shaking?"

"How'd you know it was me?"

"Caller ID, dumb-dumb."

He laughed. "Right. Listen, Al wants help down here. Big job."

"Burial ground?" she asked.

"Not sure. Lots of remains, though. How long do you think it'll take to get a team here?"

She sighed. "Got that fire on Hudson. Think it's arson.

And they just arrived at the gas station robbery on Fourth. Two dead. Suspect fled. Let's see," she made a whooshing sound. "I guess I can have five or six people there in about a half hour. New shift comes on in the morning. Can't send more until then."

"That'll have to do. Oh, and he said to send some tents too."

* * *

Jenny had seen some shit in her five years working for the Sheriff's department, but thankfully, a mass grave hadn't been one of them. This one was old, so it wasn't as disturbing, for some reason, as she figured a fresh grave might be. Still, she was relieved when the forensics team took over and she could look away from the dozens of bones poking out of the soil. The paperwork would be a nightmare.

"Do we seriously have to just stand here all night?" Ken, her partner, asked. "They're just collecting bones. One of them figures they've been here at least a hundred years. Not like we have to worry about the murderer coming back or anything."

"Have to keep the looky-loos out," Jenny said. "And they don't think it's a crime scene. They want to make sure it's not a historical landmark or something like that."

"Dead bodies are a historical landmark?"

"Well, if it's some kind of cemetery, then we can't go exhuming all the bodies. It's not right."

"Whatever. Still don't see why they need us standing around like idiots."

"How's Bailey?" she asked, knowing the question would make stop bitching about doing his job.

"All right. Wants to move in."

Bailey was a stripper Ken met when he worked the drug unit. They'd dated for about a year. Jenny still wasn't sure if Ken had feelings for the woman, or if he was just enamored by the fact he was banging a stripper.

"And?" she asked.

"I don't see why we should complicate a good thing," he said. "She's got her shit, I've got mine. Perfect as we are, in my opinion."

Jenny sighed. The wind stirred again, churning the loose dirt at the excavation site into a small cloud. It stung her eyes a little. She was glad she wasn't in there digging with the guys wearing the blue onesies. "Think we're going to get a storm."

Ken laughed. "That'll send the rats scurrying. They're still fucking around with that tent."

The wind blew again, filling her mouth with dust. Jenny coughed. "Guess we should put the masks on like they told us."

"Little bit of dirt never hurt anyone."

Jenny pulled her mask up anyway. The dust made her sinuses ache and she didn't like the idea of dead body particles blowing into her mouth.

"God, this is so boring." Ken straightened. "Want some coffee?"

"I'd love some."

"I'll be ten minutes."

"Right," she said. He'd go home, fuck around for a while, and then come back about an hour before their shift ended.

Chapter 3

Kill them all.

The thought floated around Clive's pain-riddled brain. Teasing him, terrifying him, and, most disturbingly, arousing him.

Going to the ER was a bad idea. Too many people. Babies cried. Men yelled. Somewhere a machine beeped with merciless persistence. Why didn't someone turn it off?

Sounds. Lights. Smells. People touching him. Talking to him. All of it created a cacophony of sensations that overwhelmed his brain. Combined with the fire currently burning a path from his sinuses to the back of his neck, Clive couldn't focus, and yet, at the same time, he couldn't do anything *but* focus.

"Mr. Fallow?" a woman asked. The nurse. She was nice. Gentle. But her voice stabbed his ears like sharp icicles.

Unable to speak, Clive put up a hand. Just stop. That's all he wanted. If everything just stopped, he'd hear nothing and feel nothing and it would be over. No more pain. No more strange thoughts.

But he knew that wasn't true. The headaches stayed no matter what he did or how many pills he took. It didn't matter if he turned out all the lights, blocked every sound, and lay as still as a dead man. The pain remained. Sometimes it got worse. He'd put off going to the hospital, because he'd had migraines before, and knew that little could be done about them, but these were nothing like what he'd experienced before. They came with hallucinations and urges he barely controlled.

The hospital, he decided, was the worst place he could be. Should just get up. Go home. Wait it out.

Kill himself.

"I need you to look at me, Mr. Fallow. Can you understand what I'm saying?"

He nodded. The movement rocked the fire in his head, sending it smashing against his forehead. "St..."

"I think he's having a seizure," another voice said, this one male.

"No," the woman replied. "When he came in, he said it was a headache. Migraine, to be exact."

"Could be a stroke. The symptoms are sometimes remarkably similar."

"I know, but he's got a history of migraines."

"Is he on any meds?"

"Said nothing makes it stop, so he hasn't bothered taking anything for it."

"Should run some tests anyway. Rule out a stroke. Better to err on the side of caution, right? He's insured?"

"Yes."

"Good. Maybe we could..."

Their voices blended into the tortuous sensation of the doctor's hands on his head. Pressing. Pushing. Poking.

"Stop." Clive pushed blindly at the hands. "Hurts."

"Mr. Fallow, I know this seems cruel, but I need you to look at the light."

What part of migraine did they not understand? Look at the light and sear a hole in his brain. Right. He really wanted to do that. He avoided doctors for this very reason. They thought he was exaggerating when a cluster struck. That maybe he just had a low pain tolerance or was suffering some kind of drug withdrawal. One doctor sent him for brain scans and blood tests, because she thought he was having a stroke. They always thought it was a stroke. Idiots. In the end, every time, they gave him some form of pain killer and sent him home. The meds drugged him into a brief sleep, but they did nothing to dull the pain. The headache followed him into his dreams, and continued when he woke, often more intense than before.

He took a leave from work, finally, after missing two full weeks thanks to these damn clusters. Totally fucked his internship. They might allow him to graduate anyway. Extenuating circumstance and all. Al had left a few days before him, although no one ever told him why. Just said he had some health issues and needed a break to deal with them. Maybe he was having the headaches too, which meant it was caused by something they'd encountered at work… Clive tried to grasp the thought that followed. He saw the mass grave, the dirt, and Al saying something… but it was lost.

They were always like this. Turned his brain into mush. Thoughts came but vanished before he could grasp them. This time, though, it was different. Clive felt angry. Out of control. He didn't know how he detected the difference, as the clusters often left him disoriented and unable to think clearly enough to notice anything but the pain, but he knew. The fist in his chest, roaring in his ears, and the way his muscles twitched with the desire to strike out were all new. He didn't know what he wanted to strike out at. Not like he could punch a headache.

"Okay," the woman was saying. "We'll put in an IV then?"

Silence.

"Doctor?"

"Yes," the doctor said. "Get urine and blood samples as well. He's got a fever and I don't like those welts on his skin."

The idea of them sticking him with a needle, finding a vein he already knew would be tough to find, and then wheeling him out of the ER, into the elevator, down a hallway, and to a room… Clive couldn't do it. If the pain would just stop, he could cope. If he could just hang onto a thought, maybe...

It wouldn't stop, though. Not here. Not now.

Not ever.

He opened his eyes. The fluorescent lights burned his retinas. On a small cart near the left side of the bed, he saw a tray. On top of the tray were several items, but his mind focused on the tongue depressors.

The doctor droned on, while the nurse rubbed his right arm with an alcohol swab. The cold liquid on his skin made him nauseous.

As Clive stared at the long, flat pieces of wood, rage bubbled in his lungs, heating every breath. He reached. Felt the smooth wood, closed his fingers around it, and then turned. The nurse prepped the IV needle. He only saw half of it. The dreaded aura was back in his vision, obscuring half of everything he looked at with millions of tiny lights.

Clive squeezed the tongue depressor as the nurse poked his arm. Nope. No vein. She pulled it out, tapped his arm, and then tried again. Still no vein. He lifted his hand as she leaned forward again, needle pointed at his bruised skin. As though sensing his intention, she looked up. He struck.

The warmth of her blood on his hand was soothing, but her scream tore through his brain. He tasted something metallic. The flavor made him gag, and then vomit on himself. The nurse pushed at his face, voices screeched. Hands on his arms. On his legs. More screaming. Clive still held the tongue depressor. It slid out of her eye socket as she crumpled to the floor. He stood and then pressed the bloody end against his eye as the doctor and several uniformed men circled him. Before they could stop him, Clive fell forward. The tongue depressor slipped down his cheek and into his mouth. Better. Bodies crashed into him, their weight forced his head into the wall, and drove the tongue depressor into his throat.

He choked. Falling. The thin piece of wood blocked his airway, cut at the back of his throat. Someone grabbed his face. Clive shut his mouth. Clamped his jaw tightly closed. No air. Noises blurred until they dulled to a gentle roar. Finally, darkness clouded his vision, making the aura dissipate. Pounding in his ears. Couldn't breathe... breathing was bad anyway.

The pain stopped.

* * *

"This one was part of a drug trial here at the university. He signed a form releasing his body for 'research purposes' a few months back," the orderly, Calvin, who often delivered the research cadavers to the university, seemed proud of himself. "Aren't you going to ask what drug trial?"

"The one Dr. Stevens ran for his migraine medication?"

"Damn. You're no fun."

"I can't see you bringing me a body that was testing diabetic drugs or treatments for menopause. And I thought I told you the last time you brought a cadaver that I only need the brain."

"They said the infectious diseases nerds want the rest. Already made the call. I give him to them, you might not get your brain, so I brought him here first. Avoid the brain-stealing middleman."

"I see."

"Once you take what you need, give Brenda a call and she'll send someone over to get the rest of him out of your way."

"Infectious diseases?" Morris took a step back from the gurney. "Should I be concerned?"

"Don't think so. I mean, he had something, obviously, but they stored him with the other stiffs in the morgue, so they can't be too worried about him being contagious. When I move those guys, I have to suit up and shit. No special instructions when they gave him to me."

He'd have to take precautions, just in case. If I.D.

wanted a body, then they suspected its owner died of something viral. "I don't suppose you got a file for me this time/"

"Are you kidding? No way do I want to hear another of your hissy fits." He handed Morris a white envelope. "Normally I have to chase this shit down, but the doc at the hospital practically shoved it up my ass."

"Any idea why?"

He shrugged. "Dude just lost his shit, they said. Came in for a headache, and then it was bloody bananas. Doc's probably covering his ass. Oh, and I'll need that file for Infectious Diseases, so make yourself a copy and send the original with his body."

Calvin sometimes made little sense. Morris usually found him amusing. "Got it. I hope they ran his blood and urine. It'd save me some time."

"Yep. I peeked at the file, but don't tell anyone."

Morris smiled. "I won't."

"They did a full panel. No drugs or any other chemicals in his system. Guy's had several scans done over the past couple of months, but nothing abnormal turned up."

"Thanks," Morris said. He opened the envelope. "Sometimes the problem doesn't show up on a scan. With any luck, his brain will give me a clue to why he died."

"What part of bloody bananas didn't you understand?" Calvin asked.

"I understand he attacked a nurse, but crazy isn't a diagnosis. Something had to trigger the violence."

"Attacked her with a fucking tongue depressor. And then he swallowed the damn thing and choked to death."

"Christ. That's a shitty way to go."

"The nurse survived. Lost some vision but nothing major. Guess the tongue depressor went up and behind her eyeball, but he didn't stab deeply enough to do major damage."

"Small mercies, I suppose." He read the results from the

blood tests. No virus detected.

Morris was excited about the brain now. If this were a violence-inducing cluster, it might hold more information than the regular clusters he'd studied. There'd only been one other brain he'd been able to study firsthand, but that had been a suicide. The patient lived alone, and wasn't discovered for several days, so decomposition ruined most of the tissue.

"Maybe he's got a tumor they can't see on the scans," Calvin suggested. "I hear tumors can make you all kinds of crazy."

"I doubt it. The other symptoms indicate it's the same as the other cluster patients, and we found no tumors in any of those cases."

"What are clusters?"

"Prolonged migraine headaches. We call them clusters because they last for several days, and then leave for a brief period before returning again. And I've noticed a dramatic spike in suicide headaches resulting in violence over the past few months. Wouldn't have noticed it if I weren't looking, I suppose, but my research brought it to my attention. Anyway, the data suggests the violent episodes are being caused by something chemical or environmental. Killing themselves isn't unusual, because they're desperate to stop the pain, but violence against other people is rare."

Calvin grimaced. "Well, I've gotta get back to it. Good luck. I'll call if the boss gets any other goodies at the morgue."

"Thanks again."

Calvin wheeled his gurney out as Morris finished reading the medical records for Clive Fallow, the man now laying on his table. Headaches began about five months prior to the final one. He'd have to find out what Mr. Fallow did for a living, where he'd been. He could get Rachel to work on that. He scribbled a note on the front of the envelope so he wouldn't forget to mention it when Rachel returned from lunch. Something told him this brain had the answers to the many questions he had about these new clusters. Hopefully, he could figure out where to find them.

"Well, Mr. Fallow," Morris set down the file and then picked up the bone saw. "Let's see what's been eating your brain."

CHAPTER 4

Jenny laid on the floor. The cold wood felt nice against her skin, and the hard surface sent pain to other parts of her body, which made the headache seem less intense. She moved as little as possible. If she could stop breathing, then maybe she wouldn't vomit again.

No. If she stopped breathing she'd die. Didn't want to die. Ken did that. Killed himself. Never saw that coming. If he hadn't taken sick leave, she wouldn't have had to see him like that. Rotten. Stinking. Dead.

She admitted, but only to herself, that the idea of dying, while unacceptable, held some appeal. Death meant silence. God, she'd kill anyone, even herself, for a few minutes of peace.

But death was bad. She wanted to live. Most of the time anyway.

At least her mother stopped moving around downstairs. When the headaches became bad enough for her to take a leave of absence from work, her mom insisted on staying with her. They barely got along at yearly holiday dinners, so the past three months would've been stressful without the migraines. Jenny begged her to go home. Insisted she was fine. As usual, her mother didn't listen. She rattled around Jenny's house like an annoying, concerned ghost. Flitting in and out, forcing broth and other shit into her mouth. She ignored Jenny's pleas to be left alone. Ignored her demands for quiet. Kept mothering her to death.

She told herself she should be grateful. Her mom dropped everything to be there. This last cluster brought with it a rage she'd never felt before, though, and in the darkest hours, when she thought she might die from the pain, Jenny had terrifying thoughts. Things no one should imagine doing to anyone, least of all their mother. As quickly as they came, the thoughts left. Her mind leapt from one thing to another, making it difficult to patch together a coherent internal dialogue. Speech was even more difficult.

For hours, she'd listened to her mom's shoes on the tile floors. Each step was agony. Jenny considered numerous ways to ensure she never took another step. Then, mercifully, everything went dark. She dreamed for the first time in weeks, until something woke her. The silence, she decided. She hadn't had that in... the thought disappeared.

She tugged the blanket from her bed until the soft material covered her face and neck. The sensation of cotton against her skin should've been pleasant, but it made her want to crawl out of her skin. Still, the darkness it provided and the gentle pressure on her head made the throbbing in her sinuses less intense. Trade one discomfort for another.

She closed her eyes. Bits of her dream returned. In it, she remembered walking down the stairs, approaching a shadow near the door, and then hearing her mother scream. Felt the rage blossom in her brain. It stretched downward, into her mouth, her throat, and then the tentacle-like sensation journeyed to her belly, where it wrapped itself around her organs, feeding her fury. Jenny had never experienced anything like it. Not in real life, and certainly not in a dream.

Then she remembered her mother's face. Blood covered her cheek and neck. Her eyes, blue like Jenny's, bulged in a comical way. Jenny had shoved her face away in the dream, unable to bear seeing her mother like that, but her hand slid over the blood and into a wound on her neck. She'd called 9-1-1 in the dream, but no one came.

Something wasn't...

Goosebumps erupted on her skin. She took a deep breath. Wait. She inhaled again, this time through her nose.

Nothing. No pain. No nausea. She opened her eyes. The aura was gone, although she still felt a little disoriented.

Oh, thank God, it was over. For now. She might get three or four pain free days this time. Sometimes, when the clusters lasted more than a week, the universe compensated her by giving her a day or two extra before filling her head with fire again.

She slowly rose from the floor. Every part of her body was stiff. She stretched, felt her joints crack, and her muscles heaved a sigh of relief. Still a little unsteady. Probably lack of food. Her legs felt like jelly as she carefully walked to the door.

As she put her hand on the knob, Jenny paused to examine the sticky substance that transferred to her fingers. She must be still dreaming. The headache wasn't really gone. This was her subconscious wishing it away. If she were awake, her doorknob wouldn't be covered in blood and she'd feel pain.

She opened the door, letting her dream self into the hallway, where she found more blood on the floor. Jenny walked through it, marveling at how the stickiness under her feet felt so real. She walked down the stairs, stopping halfway as a bout of dizziness overwhelmed her. When it passed, she continued to the bottom, where her mother lay on her back.

Outside, she saw lights. They flashed red and blue. That wasn't in the first dream. Had to be a new one. A part two.

She knelt next to her mother. Her bare foot bumped something. A knife. The one from the butcher block in the kitchen. Jenny picked it up. It felt heavy. She touched the end. It bit into her skin, and the pain... the pain was real.

"Oh no," she whispered as the door swung open.

Two police officers stood, guns raised, in the doorway. "Put the knife on the floor and raise your hands."

She set the knife down. "I don't know what happened. Help her."

"Ma'am, I need you to raise your hands."

Jenny did as he instructed. "Please, I don't know what happened. This isn't real."

They spoke, but she didn't hear them. The aura was back in her vision and a sharp prick of pain pierced the back of her eye. She turned the knife toward herself. A breathtaking force threw her backward before sleep reclaimed her mind.

* * *

Morris heard about the police officer from one of the nurses. He often ate his lunch in the hospital cafeteria and heard the nurse discussing the case with a coworker. The officer had some kind of episode in which she'd become violent. Killed someone before coming to her senses. Somehow, though, she'd had enough self-awareness to call for help.

Because the police officer claimed she had no memory of it, and had never harmed another person in her life, they'd admitted her for psychological evaluation rather than stuffing her in a jail cell. When the nurse mentioned a headache, his skin tingled.

Another one.

While the nurse had been a little embarrassed when he approached to say he'd overheard her conversation, she gave him Dr. Brant's cell number. A couple of calls, some cajoling, and Morris was granted a meeting with the hospital's newest migraine patient.

She sat on the corner of her bed, knees up, arms over her head. It wasn't hard to see Jenny Collins was in pain and severely depressed. Who wouldn't be after murdering someone, especially their mother?

"Miss Collins," Morris said softly. "I know the headache makes this difficult, so I'll try to be brief."

"I don't remember anything," she said. "They said I killed her, but I don't know why I would."

"I don't want to know about your mother."

She glanced at him. Her eyes were bloodshot, the pupils barely more than a pinprick in size. "Why not?"

"I want to know about the headaches."

"The other doctors couldn't stop them. I suppose you think you can?"

"I don't believe I can stop them. Yet. If I can understand what triggers them, then maybe I can figure out what made you black out and then, eventually, find a way to treat people like you."

"I think I'm long past treatment, but I'd hate to see someone else get hurt."

"So would I."

"What do you want to know?"

"How long have you suffered from migraines?"

"I've never had headaches like this in my life. The last one's almost gone now. Just a bit of pain lingering in my eyes mostly."

"When did they start?"

"About five or six months ago. I don't know for sure. Everything's still fuzzy."

Morris made notes as she talked. "Anything else happen around that time? Did you go anywhere unusual? Change in diet or environment? Did something happen at work?"

She shook her head and then took a deep breath. Squinting, she pressed her forehead before releasing the air from her lungs. "The only memorable thing I can think of is that we had to guard this excavation site. I remember it being windy and we had to wear masks. I got some dirt in my eyes and my mouth. Headache started that night, but it didn't last long. It was about a week before I got a migraine, so it's probably not relevant."

"How long did the migraine last?" Morris struggled to keep the excitement out of his voice.

"Few hours."

"Okay," he said. "How long after the excavation did the first cluster start?"

"Cluster?"

"Prolonged pain and disorientation. Anything longer than a day or two."

She shook her head. "Not sure. Couple of weeks. A month maybe."

"What were they excavating?"

"Bones."

He frowned. "Was this the mass grave they found at the shopping center lot?"

She nodded.

Clive Farrow had worked that site as well. Finally, he might have a connection. "Have they done any MRI's or bloodwork since you've been here?"

"My doctor has done all that…" she closed her eyes. "Before I k… before I lost my shit, they said they found nothing. My brain is normal."

"If you don't mind, I'd like to schedule a few more tests. We can wait until you're feeling up to it."

"Why?"

"These clusters are serious, as you know, and they can cause psychological trauma not unlike what you'd see in someone suffering from PTSD. If I can identify abnormalities in your brain, we might be able to explain what happened and find a treatment that works."

"Whatever. I don't care anymore. They should just let me die."

Morris didn't reply. What could he say to that anyway? Instead, he finished making his notes and then stood. "I want to help you, Miss Collins. What happened isn't your fault."

"If I killed her, then I deserve whatever happens to me."

"You deserve to be well," he said. "If an illness caused you to do this, you don't belong in jail."

"I don't belong on the street either."

"If I can treat it, though, you can live a full, normal life."

"No thanks."

"I'm not giving up on you."

She turned toward the wall. Morris sighed as he left the room. He'd speak to the doctor and get those tests, maybe see if Mark, a neurosurgeon he often consulted during his research, would be willing to do an exploratory surgery with Jenny's consent. Then he'd call the precinct where she worked and request a list of everyone involved in the excavation of those bones. Jenny's was the most promising case he'd seen, because she was still alive, and another link to the mass grave.

He pressed the button on the elevator door and recalled his first conversation with a new patient. Al was a crime scene investigator who mentioned working on an excavation of an old burial ground. Morris suspected Al might be a third link to that site. Should call and make sure he's okay. Maybe warn him about the potential for a violent episode. He might even be able to convince Al to admit himself so Morris could observe him and to make sure no one else got hurt.

Morris got into the elevator with a hop in his step. Maybe he'd stumbled on some type of virus. The attention garnered from being on the ground floor of a new disease discovery might provide enough steam to get his migraine research some desperately needed funding.

Not that he was happy about a mystery illness that made people homicidal. Money was money, though, and he'd take it however he could get it.

* * *

The room was familiar. He couldn't remember why, though. Was it his bedroom? Someone else's? Why would he be in someone else's room? That was sil—the thought vanished. Must be in his own bed. Felt like his bed.

He winced as another burst of flames lanced his brain. It settled behind his eyes, but now and then, it whipped its tail all the way to the back of his neck. Why couldn't he see properly? The strange prism-like lights over his right eye made him feel a little nauseous. The experience wasn't new, but it was. His throat constricted, like he might cry, but then something told him it'd be okay. He'd done this before. If he just relaxed, everything would be fine. He just needed—not sure what.

Something.

He lay on the bed, knowing he should get up. Take a painkiller, maybe, and figure out whose house he was in.

"Al?" the voice calling him may as well be a bomb, its effect on his headache was similar to that of his head exploding. "Al, you getting up or what?"

Yes, he was Al. Or... the thought disappeared as soon as it came. He felt so... what's the word? He grabbed at it, but tiny bits of angry in his brain spirited it away. Now that thought was ridiculous.

"Hey," the voice was close. "Oh, honey. Still got a migraine? I wish you'd make an appointment. It could be another cluster. They said if you got one, they needed to observe it."

A cluster was bad. He didn't know how he knew that, but he did. "They" were also bad. Why, though? Because *they* were unknown, probably. Never trust what you don't know.

He opened his eyes. A woman with freckled skin and brown eyes leaned over him. Her dark hair was familiar. He knew the lines around her mouth like he knew the backs of his own hands. Wait, he didn't remember his hands. Were they—?

"Al!"

Christ. That voice. It burned his retinas. Retinas... he felt like he appreciated the word. Was appreciated a correct description? It all felt foreign; the words, thoughts, sounds. Should make it stop. No time for thinking. Just sleeping.

"Hey, hon," she said. "Look at me."

She was Laaaaa... again, the word disappeared. Her name was there. It floated around his head, but he couldn't catch it long enough to know it.

"Al! Come on, sweetie. Look at me. Try to focus."

He closed his eyes again. "Please go," he tried to say, but he knew it didn't come out right. Was he dying? He wished it would happen already.

"You're late for work," she said. "Aren't you going back today? You were so excited last night."

Work sounded familiar too. He should know what that was, but the word was no more than a sound. Letters strung together without meaning or effect. *Wooorrrrk*. He had a feeling he didn't like whatever work was.

"I'm calling the doctor."

Good. Do that. He was so tired.

No, wait. The doctor. An invisible fist clutched his chest. It squeezed the bits and pieces inside until he couldn't breathe. His only thought, his only instinct, was to avoid going to this doctor.

Legs moved. Body forced itself to a seated position. The room spun a little, but he managed to get to his feet. Her voice carried down the... uh... the space outside the door. Again, another word he can't grasp.

"Yeah," she said into the phone. "He hasn't gotten out of bed in two days. Speech is slurred. Seems to be disoriented too. I don't think he knows who I am." She sounded upset, but he knew it was a ploy. Wanted to get rid of him. "You said the drugs were working." Silence. "Well, they stopped working. This one's just as bad as the last one. Maybe worse."

Whatever it was causing these headaches, it wasn't good. Al had enough medical knowledge to know migraines like these don't just start out of the blue and for no reason. They said there were no tumors, but he felt something in there. It moved now and then. Seared a path from his sinus to a spot just behind his right eye, before burrowing itself back in his sinus again.

He told them to check his nose. They did. Said nothing was there. Liars. Something was crawling around in there. A worm or a bug. They'd see those. Could be mold spores.

32 CLUSTER

Where would he have inhaled a spore?

The bones... he dug for the thought, but it drifted away as another sharp pain lanced through his eye.

He should just kill himself. Be done with it.

Where did that thought come from? A part of him knew it wasn't rational, but another part, a louder part, said it might be. He walked into the darkness beyond the door.

She... he knew her, but didn't know who she was, stood at the top of the stairs, phone to her ear.

She's the real problem here. Always dragging you outside, making everything worse.

"Hey, Al," she said. "They're sending an ambulance. You should lie down."

Al. That was him. He was Al. Had to be. He blinked. The aura of prisms had expanded, now obscuring most of the ride side of his vision. His cheek felt numb as well, and his tongue felt foreign... like it belonged to someone else.

He took a step, and then one more. Hand on her head. He pushed.

She drifted for a moment, like a leaf caught in a gust of wind. And then she screamed. Gravity took her. He covered his ears. The sound of her terror sparked an electric jolt deep in his brain. She was gone. His Laura. That's her name. He stared at the space before him. Opened his arms. Leaned forward.

*   *   *

"How's the headache research going?" Sharon asked.

"It'd go faster if you didn't interrupt me." Morris placed the sample on the slide and then carefully pressed another on top. "Did Tony get the algorithm done? If not, I know you know better than to pester me."

"Mind like yours should be curing diseases like cancer, Mo, not finding the cure for a headache."

"Migraine clusters," he corrected. "Which can be as deadly and as terrifying as cancer."

"Deadly? Unless it's a tumor, I think you're being a little dramatic. Headaches won't kill you."

"First of all, the cases I'm studying aren't just headaches. The pain is extraordinary. Some sufferers describe it as worse than childbirth, to give you perspective. Now, imagine the worst pain you've ever experienced. No medication alleviates it, and it returns several times a day for a week or more. Suddenly, without reason, it stops. You know it's going to happen again, because it always does, but you don't know when.

"Other symptoms are happening with the pain too, like this guy," he pointed to the slide, "had prisms of light in his vision, numbness and disorientation. He also mentally disconnected from everything around him. Imagine knowing that what you're experiencing isn't new, but not being able to grasp why or what it is. He'd slip into an amnesiac state. Couldn't tell you his name. Didn't know his own wife."

"Still, not deadly."

He sighed. "But they become deadly, because they mess with your mind. Some people have these headaches at least once a day for a year at a time. Every single day. Imagine that for a second. Pain you can't stop every single day for hundreds of days. They become depressed, anxious, angry even. Eventually, the only thought is how to make it stop. That's why they're referred to as suicide headaches."

"Okay," she said. "Why not put them on a steady dose of painkillers? I'm sure modern medicine has something strong enough to treat the pain."

"There probably is something strong enough, but those meds are highly addictive."

"True, but the pain would be gone, so with supervision, a patient could be weaned off eventually."

"And what about the other symptoms?"

"I imagine once the pain is gone, the other symptoms would be a non-issue."

Morris shook his head. "Most patients will tell you that

the pain is a minor issue. It's the other stuff that drives them mad."

"Maybe diet or environment could be adjusted to treat the symptoms. I've heard fantastic things about oxygen therapy."

"There have been minor improvements with dietary modifications, but so far, clusters are untreatable. Generally, it's a rare condition, and sufferers harm no one but themselves. However, I've noticed a spike in violent behavior toward others in patients that never had these headaches before. Weirdest part is they're localized."

"What do you mean?"

"I've only been able to find cases in this county, and the first of them seem to date back almost exactly six months."

"What is it you think Tony can do? He's a tech guy."

"With the right algorithm, I might be able to organize the data so I can identify a connection between them."

"Such as?"

"Common event or environmental factors. Maybe genetic ties. I don't know. If I can isolate what makes these brains different from those who suffer from non-violent clusters, then a treatment won't be far behind."

"What if there is nothing to find?"

"Has to be. The localization and timing isn't a coincidence."

"Okay," she straightened. "Maybe you're on to something. I'll give Tony a nudge so he prioritizes your request."

"Thank you."

"You still coming to Jay's?"

He forgot about agreeing to go for drinks. Someone, he wasn't sure who, was retiring. "Maybe. Just want to get some preliminary tests done on this sample."

"So that's a no."

She didn't wait for an answer. He watched her leave the lab, phone in her hand. Once upon a time, he and Sharon had been sort of in love. She hated the hours he put into his work, though, and the romantic element in their relationship fizzled. Now they were just friends. Most of the time.

Morris put the slide under the microscope. His work was more important than relationships that probably wouldn't last. If he could stop one person from dying like Al had, then he had to keep looking for at least a cause. Find the cause, the solution is never far behind.

Al's case had stumped him. He'd suffered so intensely for weeks, Morris was sure he'd had a tumor. The test results said he was wrong, but he was hopeful. At least Al wanted to find out why the headaches plagued him and did whatever Morris asked in the name of research.

When he later discovered that Clive and Jenny had also been at the excavation of the bones, he'd requested a list of all personnel assigned to the dig. Then his assistant, Rachel, gathered a list of ER patients complaining of headaches over the past six months, and they matched several names to the list. Clive's violent outburst wasn't necessarily a suicide, but Morris suspected he wanted to die. Ken, Jenny's partner, killed himself with his service weapon. Jenny cut her mother's throat. Definitely a pattern. Too bad the rest of them weren't willing to come in for testing. Al was the only one, so far, willing to participate in the study.

He should've asked him to continue his weekly visits, but he went into a remission period and Morris figured there would be nothing to study. He told Al to come in if he experienced new symptoms.

Al didn't call for a couple of weeks. When the symptoms returned, he snapped. Killed his wife and then himself.

A spark of guilt burned his brain. He should've known better. Should've monitored Al despite the loss of symptoms.

Morris shook off the uncomfortable feelings of shame and self-doubt and peered into the microscope. The tissue looked normal. He increased the magnification. On the right side of the sample, a thin line wriggled. Morris stepped back.

Maybe his fatigue overwhelmed his common sense. He didn't just see an organism moving through the tissue. Couldn't have. He'd examined Al's brain so many times, he'd have seen it before.

Taking a breath, Morris looked through the lens again. There it was. Thin, slightly darker than the surrounding tissue, and moving rapidly in a circular pattern. Was that a...?

He put his finger on the slide, meaning only to nudge it to the left a little bit, but it slipped and the slide fell. Morris caught it but cracked the center.

"Shit." He carefully set the pieces back on the microscope and looked again.

Nothing. Whatever had been there, was gone. He eyed the desk. Probably dead now. Fuck. It might have left behind clues, though. Proteins or cells. Excitement fluttered in his chest.

"Hey," Sharon called from the doorway.

He turned, pushing his glasses upward so he could see her face. "What?"

"We're leaving in an hour. Just in case you get bored with your brains."

Maybe a break as a good idea. He'd come back with fresh eyes and avoid more stupid mistakes like not securing his slides properly. Morris nodded. "Can I get a ride with you?"

"Really?"

"Yeah. I've had enough for one day."

"Sure."

"Just let me get cleaned up. I'll meet you downstairs."

Chapter 5

"I can't explore someone's brain without a reason," Mark said. "Jesus, Mo. You know better."

Morris picked at the edge of the file Mark handed back to him after reading the first page. "The reason is she experiences pain so excruciating that she becomes a different person."

"She's had MRI's. Nothing shows up."

"Exactly."

"No, Mo. I'm not doing it."

"She's consented. I don't see the issue."

"The issue is that opening her head to take a gander at her brain is ridiculous, because I don't even know what I'm looking for. It's invasive and unnecessary."

"I saw something in a patient presenting the same symptoms. A parasite, I think."

"Where is it?"

"Where's what?"

Mark sighed. "The parasite."

"I lost it."

"You're smart, Mo. Too smart to be wasting your time in a university lab studying headaches."

"Your point?"

"You're not challenged in there. Got your head so far in the clouds, you can't even keep track of a parasite."

"My head was where it should be. I forgot to secure the slide is all. Just a simple, albeit stupid, mistake anyone could've made." Morris shrugged. "Look, I know what I saw. I'm running tests now to see if it left any traces in the tissue and after interviewing most of the crew that excavated the burial site, I discovered at least half are suffering headaches. Three have had violent episodes, and two committed suicide. That's too coincidental for me. There's something wrong and the only one willing to let us open them up is Jenny. Come on. Can't you use a scope or something? You don't have to be invasive."

Mark scowled. "Okay, so let's say I do it. What am I looking for?"

"A parasite."

"I know that. Any particular kind? Will it be visible to the naked eye or is it microscopic?"

"I'm thinking it could be Toxoplasmosis."

"That infects rodents, not people."

"Yeah, but what's interesting is how it affects their brains. Makes them lose their fear of cats. Actually, they're attracted to cat urine for some reason. So, naturally, they get eaten or killed by a cat, the parasite reproduces in the cat's digestive tract, and then the cycle repeats."

"Still not seeing why you think this is what's inside a human brain."

"This parasite can and has infected humans. Studies have shown it's unusually common in schizophrenics."

"Studies, eh?"

"I can get the literature for you. Mind you, the results are inconclusive, but the dots are there. All we need are a few more lines to connect them."

"We could do a contrast first," he said. "Maybe a biopsy, if the results show reason to do it."

Morris would take what he could get. "Okay. I'll just have to hope it gives us something."

"Tell your patient to make an appointment with Sally."

"Uh, she's already in the hospital."

"Is it that bad?"

"She's on four."

Mark pressed his forehead. "Psych?"

"Yes. Killed her mother."

"Is she even able to give consent?"

"Yes, she's very lucid, most of the time. I had her psychiatrist write a letter detailing this. We're covered."

"Fine. You make the arrangements. I'm not opening her up, though. Not yet."

"So... what are you doing then?"

"A few tests. If I see something, then we'll talk."

"Sure. Thanks, Mark. I really appreciate it."

"I bet. Now, get out of here. Some of us have patients to see."

Morris left Mark's office feeling only slightly optimistic. If the parasite absorbed dye, they might see it. If it was in the right place during the scan, they may be able to pull it out with a biopsy. So many ifs. For Jenny's sake, he hoped at least one of them worked out.

* * *

It took a couple of hours to finish Jenny's scan, because she seemed unable to remain still for more than a few seconds. They sedated her. While she didn't sleep exactly, she didn't move as much, which was good enough. Mark said nothing as he put the films on the lighted board. Morris remained silent as well as he stared at each one.

The first showed a normal brain. In the second image, though, he saw what he suspected all along.

"See that?" Morris pointed to the elongated shadow near the base of Jenny's brain.

"Yeah. What is it?"

"I think it's my parasite."

Mark looked at the remaining images. He pointed to the fourth one. "Look. It's changed position here. It looks almost... worm-like."

Morris's heart pounded. Finally. "And here," he pointed to the sixth image. "It's moved up. Looks larger too."

"Could be more than one."

"Think so?"

"Only way to explain how it's doubled in size in a matter of seconds."

"Reproducing or were there more than one to begin with?"

"That is a very good question," Mark said. "Okay, Mo. You win. I'll see what's open and get her in as soon as possible."

"I'm not sure what kind of defense mechanisms it has, so I don't think removing it would be wise. It could release a toxin, which might kill her."

"Then how are you going to test it?"

"Can you remove the brain tissue around it? Take the parasite without letting it know it's being removed?"

Mark shrugged. "Depends on where it is. There are other methods that don't involve removing bits of brain. If I anesthetize the tissue, the parasite may be affected long enough to remove it before it can defend itself. I'll talk it over with Mary in Infectious Diseases. See what she thinks is the best approach."

"Thanks, Mark. I better get Jenny's paperwork started."

As Morris headed downstairs, he tried to contain his excitement. They weren't out of the woods yet. They had to catch the little bastard.

His phone vibrated against his thigh. Morris took it out of his pocket and then touched the screen. "Hello."

"Hey, Mo," Rachel said. "Got those test results back on your brain tissue."

Al's brain. He'd sent samples to another lab to make sure he hadn't been imagining things when he found those eggs. "Yeah? Can you give me a summary?"

"Sure. Looks like they found eggs they can't identify. Not human or from any parasite we've encountered."

"I knew it."

"You sound a little too happy, Mo. This is a parasite we're talking about."

"Sorry. It's a lead and I don't have many of those."

"I get it. Oh, and they said it's unidentified."

"Pardon?"

"Well, I told them your hypothesis that it's Toxoplasmosis or something related, but they say no. Definitely not."

Damn it. Still, a lead was a lead, even if it cut off one of the many possible roads he could get lost on. "I'll be there in about fifteen minutes. Could you pull Al's file for me?"

"Sure. What are you thinking?"

"Not sure yet. I need to identify those eggs if we're dealing with a new parasite. This is huge."

"Sure, everyone loves a whole new disease without a cure."

Yeah, not so good. Morris took a deep breath and then released it slowly. "One step at a time. No need to panic."

"Who's panicking? I just lose my shit every time I get a headache these days. Thanks for that."

Morris chuckled. So did he, and he had a lot of them lately. "I don't think it's airborne, whatever it is, or we'd have a lot more cases."

"Oh, lucky for us."

"To be honest, I was hoping I'd missed something. Maybe it's a new strain of *Taenia solium* or something like it."

"What's that?"

"Shame on you, Rachel. We covered this in your first year."

"Hey, I've had a lot of information dumped on me in the past four years. Give me a break."

He sighed. "It's a tapeworm found in pork. Humans contract it when the eggs contaminate the meat after slaughter. The tapeworm eggs hatch inside the human body, enter the bloodstream, and end up in the brain. They cause the formation of cysts, though, which we'd see."

"Do they cause headaches?"

"Yes, and seizures. Behavioral changes too. If left untreated, the infection can lead to death."

Rachel sighed. "I'm learning so many fun new things today, like why I'll never eat pork again."

"It's extremely rare in North America."

"Don't care."

He laughed. "I thought maybe it could be *Loa loa* too, but you can rest easy, because that one is usually found in Africa."

"Do I even dare to ask?"

"It's a parasite usually found in the eye. Makes the eye itchy and can cause the sensation of something crawling around the tissues. Over time, it can lead to damage to the nervous system and retina. Goes into the brain, where if enough of the larvae die, they can block capillaries."

"Which could cause encephalopathy, and that explains your memory issues, personality changes and headaches."

"Sort of, but not entirely. It's not transmittable. Plus, the parasite has never been visible in the eye. I've never seen anything like what came up on Jenny's scans, to be honest."

"Okay, I'll get some new tissue samples ready. No point in hypothesizing anything until we get a good look at it."

"I did see one in Al's tissue sample, but I lost it too quickly to examine it properly."

"Was it round, flat, tape, hook, hair or fluke?"

"Not sure. Definitely not round."

"There's a start. As you keep telling me, rule out what it isn't, and you're that much closer to determining what it is."

Morris smiled. "Right. Thanks, Rachel. See you soon." He ended the call as he reached the main doors of the hospital.

CHAPTER 6

Morris didn't get much from his exploration of Al's brain. He stared at the test results the lab sent him. Al's brain tissue definitely contained eggs. So, where were they?

"You busy?" Rachel asked. She stood in the doorway, folder tucked under her arm.

"No. Come in. Grab a mask. I hope you have good news for me."

She picked up a mask from the box next to the door and then put it on. "It took some digging, but I think I've got something on the origin of the parasite."

"You're my new favorite person."

"Don't get too excited. It's not exactly conclusive. More like another theory."

Morris pressed his temples. It was just a headache. To be safe, he'd scheduled a scan with Mark after lunch. It'd be nothing, but he'd feel better knowing that for sure. "What have you found?"

"Well," she said as she opened the laptop. "The land they found those bones on belonged to the Baker family until 1956. It used to be a plantation, and the Bakers were one of the wealthiest families in the county. In 1848, though, some kind of illness swept the property. Everyone, from William Baker, the head of the family, down to the boy that cleaned out the stables, started suffering from intense headaches."

Morris forgot about the throbbing in his head. "Did they determine what caused them?"

44   CLUSTER

"That's where it gets interesting. Actually, it gets interesting even before that. I pulled all newspaper clippings, journals, and whatever I could find online from this county in 1848, and apparently, there were lights in the sky a few months before the headaches started. In the morning, they found a swath of fields burned up where the lights appeared. The family replanted after doing whatever farmers do to rectify burned soil, and their crops did better than they ever had."

"Lights," Morris said. "Like *UFO* lights?"

She shrugged. "Just said a plethora of blue lights, followed by a massive boom. No mention of fire, although I assume since they found the burned field, there must have been. Could've been a meteor or something."

"Anything else?"

"Well, the local doctor tried to treat them, but he fell ill. Their pastor tried to exorcise them, but of course, no luck there either. In the end, they rounded the whole plantation up, locked them in the house, and burned it to the ground."

"What?"

"Yeah. Extreme, but they thought they were dealing with demons. The ones infected with the headaches committed murder, suicide and did all kinds of strange things. William Baker's wife smothered all her children. That's part of a neighbor's journal I found at the historical society. The neighbor's husband was so horrified by it that he left the county soon after the fire. The plantation was passed down to William Baker's cousin, who rebuilt, but the family was still plagued with strange behavior, suicides and illness."

"Odd." Morris didn't know what to do with the information. It was good, though, because they had a starting point, and the link between the clusters now and the ones then was impossible to ignore. "And what about after the property left the Baker family?"

"Not a lot of information after that, aside from deeds and the occasional news article, because people don't journal much anymore, I guess. I know one family living in the home, which was rented out by a real estate corporation, died in a murder-suicide pact of some kind. Another man, who purchased the home in 1978, hung himself. He had no family. And the last fire, which was eight years ago, was deliberately set. No one rebuilt after that. It's been vacant. Went into foreclosure, county took it over, and that's it."

"And the county sold it to a corporation, rezoned it as commercial, and they started digging for the mall. Considering our housing situation, it'd make more sense for them sell it to someone who might build apartments on the property."

She snorted. "Would you live on a property with that history?"

"People tend to ignore such things, particularly when they're homeless."

"Pretty hard to ignore."

Morris didn't believe in ghosts or curses, but Rachel might be on to something. Could be something in the soil, but what would make so many people sick in such a short span of time? He had one sample, which wasn't even large enough to test, and an MRI that told them nothing except there was an anomaly in Jenny's brain: a worm-shaped anomaly.

"What am I supposed to do with this?" he asked, although he didn't expect an answer. "I know there's a parasite of some kind infecting people, but I can't prove it. I can't even convince my test subjects that there's something in their brain making them sick."

"You've got Al's tissue and Jenny's scans."

"I've got the test results on Al's tissue. The tissue itself is giving me nothing."

"They found eggs."

"Yea, but the problem is the eggs deteriorate rapidly, apparently, so by the time I got around to testing the tissue a third time, the eggs and all traces of the parasite were gone."

"That's weird."

"It is."

"You think it's alien? Those lights seem to be the trigger."

"Aliens are fiction. If it was a meteor that caused the fire, then maybe something in the rock transferred into the soil."

"Or something put there by aliens."

"Okay, Rachel. You can go now."

"Maybe they'll let you take a soil sample from the site." She closed the laptop and stood. "I know you're all scientific and shit, but try to look at the facts, Mo. This is not normal. Everything is pointing toward supernatural, and I think it's a mistake to ignore that. Consider that there could be other forces at work here. You say aliens are fiction. I say it's illogical to believe that humans are the only intelligent life in the galaxy."

"And my colleagues will laugh me out of the university."

"Just open your mind a little, is all I'm saying. Think outside the box. Maybe you'll hit on a solution."

The pain in his head intensified. Morris pulled out the pill bottle he'd tucked into his pocket that morning and opened the lid. He shook out two tablets and then swallowed them before replying. "An extraterrestrial parasite?"

"Stranger things have happened."

"True, but if I buy into that theory, we're truly fucked. I have no clue how to treat that."

She tapped the laptop. "But you do know how to put it to rest."

"What do you mean?"

"It was dormant for decades before they dug up that soil, because everyone infected was dead. Just saying."

He stared. No way he was going to kill people. It was insane.

CHAPTER 7

No one used the tiny office at the back of the lab, except to store files and supplies. Morris went in to get sanitizer and file boxes, but he stayed because the silence made the pounding in his head subside. He sat at the desk, light off, and enjoyed the quiet for several minutes before his thoughts turned to the parasite.

What if Mark couldn't locate it when he opened Jenny up or it disappeared like the eggs? Still had the scans and the test results from Al's tissue. That proved something other than a typical migraine cluster was going on. Without the parasite itself, though, he couldn't treat those infected by it. Could try antibiotics used against known parasites. That might work.

And if it doesn't?

He'd call the CDC. Be responsible. Get them to come in, identify the parasite, or at least determine whether it's a threat or not, and they'll take the heat for suggesting it's not of this world. Better to fuck up his study than risk any more lives.

Morris clutched his forehead. The headache intensified during his brain scan, although Mark said he saw nothing in the images. Could be psychosomatic. He wasn't usually suggestible, but the past couple of weeks had been intense. Maybe…

The thought disappeared. Morris grasped at it, but the effort caused the pain in his head to sharpen. He let it go. Probably not important anyway.

The ticking of the clock on the wall above the door

reminded him that Jenny had been in surgery for almost an hour. Mark promised to call when he was through. The entire OR and the rooms outside had been quarantined as a precaution. Mark didn't believe the parasite was easily passed from person to person, but thankfully, he'd humored Morris's paranoia and promised everyone would wear special suits and masks and would be "decontaminated" before leaving. Hopefully, it was enough.

He laid his head on the desk and closed his eyes. A little nap would probably help.

They're all going to die.

Morris kept his eyes closed. The voice wasn't real. Just fatigue making him a little loopy. By the time he woke, Jenny would be out of surgery and he'd have some answers.

* * *

Rachel didn't usually visit the ER, but she had asked one of her friends, Maya, a triage nurse, to call her if any migraine cases came in. At a little after noon, she did.

"Hey, Rachel," Maya said. "Got a migraine for you."

"Is it a cluster?"

"I think so."

"What are the symptoms?"

"Uh, maybe you should just come over. You at the lab?"

"I am. Give me twenty minutes?"

"He's in handcuffs, so we've got all the time in the world."

"Why?"

"Because he's not going anywhere."

Rachel laughed. "I mean why the cuffs?"

"Oh, went batshit on the subway. Cops said he has to be restrained for everyone's safety."

Sounded exactly like Morris's study patients. "Okay, I'll be right over."

Rachel tried to call Morris, but he didn't answer, so she

went on her own. Morris trusted her to gather data. She didn't really need him there to do that, although she'd bet he would want to talk to the patient. If he weren't carted off to jail, Morris could talk to the guy later.

Maya waited at the doors when Rachel arrived at the hospital. As she followed Maya to the man's room, she noticed another man being rushed down the hall on a gurney. Bandages covered his eyes and they'd restrained his arms and legs. Still, he screamed something unintelligible and thrashed around.

"What happened to that guy?"

"I'll find out," Maya said. "Here's the one I was telling you about."

Rachel walked into the room. One bed was occupied by a large man with bright orange hair and a gash along the side of his face. A dirty bandage circled his neck. He stared at the ceiling, but the fingers of his right hand twitched, as though trying to grasp something. "He sedated?"

"Yeah. Enough to knock down a horse. Won't sleep, though. Just goes into this trance. Sometimes he moans or says shit that doesn't make sense."

"Like?"

"Oh, you know," Maya shrugged. "They're coming. The chosen will rise. Blah, blah, rantings of a lunatic, blah."

Rachel shivered. "He said he had a headache?"

"A coworker who came in with him said he'd been sick off and on for months and complained about severe headaches. I asked where he worked."

"And?"

"He's with the Historical Society."

Rachel's heart fluttered. "Was he at the construction site where they found those bones?"

"Don't know, but I can find out. His colleague is downstairs now, waiting for the wife to arrive."

"Please do that," Rachel said. "Thanks."

"Oh, and the coworker said he tried to off himself a few

weeks ago. Cut his own throat."

"Jesus."

"Yeah. Didn't cut deep enough for it to be fatal. The doctor treating him told me that cluster headaches can really mess with your head, and that they probably prescribed him antidepressants. I haven't got his chart from his GP yet, so I can't tell you what they gave him."

"Mo says cluster migraines can be excruciating, and nothing stops the pain. It makes the patient feel isolated, because no one understands the severity of their discomfort."

"So, they become depressed."

She nodded. "It's a common side effect. I don't think they consciously choose death, though. It's more like they just want to make the pain go away."

"Different kind of pain, but same result."

"I guess."

"Does it sound like one of your cases?"

"Yeah, it does. And if he worked that site, I think we might have another link in the pattern Mo's been tracking."

"Hey," a nurse peeked around the doorway. "You Rachel Swann?"

Rachel nodded.

"We're looking for Doctor Jenkins. You're his intern, right?"

"Assistant," she corrected. "He should be in the lab."

"Nope."

Rachel sighed. "What do you need?"

"One of his patients is in the OR," she frowned. "I don't know how to explain this. There's been a complication."

"What kind of complication?"

"You should call the surgeon. I'm not sure what happened. They asked me to track Doctor Jenkins down. The service gave me your name when I couldn't reach him."

Rachel nodded. Jenny was supposed to be in surgery this afternoon. Where the hell was he? "I have to find Mo, so if you could email this guy's chart to me, that'd be great."

"I'm not supposed to do that," Maya said.

Rachel winked. "I won't tell a soul if you don't."

She glanced at the guy in the bed. "Okay, but if it gets out, I'm saying you hijacked my email."

"I think they call it hacking."

"You know what I mean."

"I know. That other guy we saw—"

"I'll find out his deal and send you his chart too. You owe me, though."

"I know," Rachel said. "I guess the next girls' night is on me?"

"I could lose my job for this, so the next ten are on you."

* * *

Morris didn't answer her calls. She texted, left three voicemails, but got nothing. When she called Mark, the surgeon, to find out what was happening, he told Rachel to just come upstairs. She had no idea what she might find, but the scene before her certainly wouldn't have crossed her mind.

"What the fuck?" she whispered.

Mark leaned on the sink behind him. He wore clean scrubs, but she noticed streaks of blood on his neck and chin. "That's what I said when it exploded. Never seen anything like it in the fifteen years I've been practicing medicine. It was almost like the parasite triggered the whole thing as a self-preservation response."

"Her brain just..."

"Yep. I went in, found the parasite almost immediately, and it stayed completely still until I tried to pull it out. Disappeared before I could grab it. A few seconds after that, her brain started swelling and then pop! The force of it even cracked the skull. I've got everyone in quarantine, because I have no idea where the parasite went or how it's transmitted. We all had bits and blood all over our scrubs. We weren't wearing gear that protected us from exploding organs. Just masks, gowns and gloves."

"I thought you guys were supposed to wear the suits."

"You ever tried to perform brain surgery in just latex gloves?"

"No, because I'm not a surgeon."

"It's hard enough to be precise with my bare hands. Add a bulky suit and the thick gloves Mo wanted me to wear, and I might as well be working with a handful of thumbs."

"Never thought about that."

He sighed. "He warned me it might have a defense mechanism, but Christ, I never imagined this."

"I don't think Mo did either."

"That's not the worst part."

God, she wasn't sure she wanted to know.

Mark straightened. "I know he's going to kill me for it, but I called the feds."

"The what?"

"CDC."

Morris would not be happy. Shit. "How long before they arrive?"

"Probably not until tomorrow morning. They want anyone suffering the same symptoms quarantined immediately. I had to shut down the entire surgical ward. No electives until they give me the green light."

She stared at the bloody glass partition. Through it, she could see the bed, Jenny's body, and bits of brain and skull scattered over the blood-soaked sheets and the floor. Thankfully, they'd covered her with a sheet. "I'll find Mo and tell him."

"I wouldn't have called without discussing it with him, but it's out of control. Brains shouldn't explode like that."

"I know."

"And tell him that while we were getting the quarantine set up for my staff, I got a call from the ER."

"More migraine cases?"

"How'd you know?"

"I was in the ER visiting one when your nurse tracked me down. They'll be quarantined too, I imagine?"

"Yes. They're running tests now, but Doctor Welsh thinks it's some kind of encephalopathy causing the violent outbursts."

"And we know the patients from Mo's study suffer the same symptoms."

"To be honest, I think we've got a potential epidemic."

"And I'm going to pray you're wrong."

"Me too," Mark said. He rubbed his forehead.

"Headache?"

"Fuck, I hope not."

* * *

"Mo!"

Something pushed against the sides of his head. Morris brushed it away.

"Mo!"

Rachel.

Why was she squeezing his head?

"Fuck off," he said, but it sounded strange to his ears. Like he mumbled it or something.

"Hey! Get up. This is bad."

Bad... yeah, it's bad. Excruciating. Morris lifted his head slowly, breathing deeply as the pain reached out from his temples, down his neck, expanding until it settled between his shoulders. He opened his desk drawer, fumbled around for a second, and then felt the bottle of painkillers he'd stashed weeks before. The lid refused to open.

"Help."

"Jesus," Rachel took the bottle. "You look like shit."

"Flu," he said. "Probably shouldn't sleep on the desk."

She laughed. "No, that always makes you a little bitchy. Here. You need to take better care of yourself. Did you even go home last night?"

"Yeah." Rachel placed a tablet in his palm. Morris shook his head. "More."

A sigh. Another tablet. That'd have to do for now. He swallowed them and then waited.

"So, Mark's been trying to reach you," Rachel said. "How long have you been in here?"

"What time?" Words hurt. They didn't even feel like words. Just sounds. Burning, awful sounds.

"It's seven."

He'd slept five hours? Shit. The pain in his head began to dull. It moved out of his back and neck, but it refused to budge from his temples. "Okay. What's the problem?"

"It's about your patient."

"Jenny?"

"Yes. Mark said they were doing fine. Skull open, brain visible and all that."

Her voice was like a jackhammer. Morris tried not to let the anger that tugged at his throat get to his mouth. Not her fault he felt like shit.

"Mark said he saw the parasite," Rachel continued. "Got ready to remove it, and then it vanished."

"Fuck," Morris said. "I should've known we wouldn't be able to extract it. Lucky we found it at all."

"But then her brain started to swell."

Oh no...

"Mark did everything he could," Rachel said. "He said the tissue just wouldn't stop swelling."

"Is she dead?"

"Her fucking brain exploded."

Morris looked up. Rachel's cheeks, normally a pretty pink, were as white as her lab coat. "Did you go up there?"

"Yeah," she said. "When Mark couldn't find you, he asked me to come up since I've been assisting with your research. I went in and," she shuddered. "I hope I never see anything like that again."

Shit. "Did you wear a mask? Tell me you wore a mask."

"Not at first."

"Shit. Rachel, you know better."

"I'm okay. I didn't go into the OR."

His thoughts were still fuzzy. It was hard to hold onto the information Rachel gave him. He took a breath, and then one more.

"Christ, I don't think anyone wants to go in there," she said.

"Where?"

"The OR."

"Right. Why not?"

"Jesus, Mo. How many painkillers have you taken? I just told you her brain *exploded*."

"So..."

"Looks like a damn crime scene."

"Oh." The throbbing in his head slowed. Maybe the headache was going away. This wasn't a cluster like the others. Just stress. Morris allowed himself to relax. "Where's Mark now?"

"Well," Rachel said. "He put everyone who was in the room in quarantine, including himself, and he called the CDC."

"Fuck." There goes his research.

"He's really sorry, Mo. He tried to avoid it, but they had two more cluster patients in the ER too. One of them killed some guy on the subway. The other one tried to carve his own eyes out."

"Shit."

"Yeah, and they were part of the team that worked at that lot digging up those bones. Considering what you've found in your research and what we saw today, I think he did the right thing."

Morris nodded. The headache was almost entirely gone and he could think again. "You did good. I was going to call them anyway. This is way over my head now."

CHAPTER 8

Morris felt good. A full night of sleep, on top of sleeping the afternoon away, and he woke with no pain. He remembered fearing the worst yesterday and laughed at himself. He had no aura, no speech distortion, so obviously what he had wasn't a migraine. After a quick shower and a cup of coffee, he drove to Rachel's apartment. Her car had been "in the shop" for two months. Morris had offered to drive her to work until it was repaired. Sometimes he regretted the offer.

Rachel met him outside, and they drove into work together. The whole way there, a twenty-two-minute drive, she talked. And talked. Morris nodded in the right places, and answered now and then, but added little to the conversation. He suspected Rachel knew he wasn't really listening. It had become part of their routine.

"I called to check on those migraine patients while I was waiting for you," she said.

"I wasn't that late."

"Thirty-five minutes, but who's counting, right?"

"You, apparently."

"Anyway, Maya said the CDC guys are at the lab now," she said, finally finding something to pique his interest. "Been there all night. A woman, can't remember her name, but she's tall and blonde, like a supermodel, but anyway, she said she'd stop by the lab around ten today to pick up your files."

"What?" He had no intention of giving up his files.

"Well, they're taking over now, so…"

"I'll give them copies. That's it. Did you talk to her? Did you tell your friend not to give them anything?"

"No. Maya didn't come with them. They put her in quarantine with the ER staff. I spoke to the CDC lady, and she asked where to find the research. I said it was probably locked in your office, so they'd have to wait until you got there. Then she said she'd be back after ten, so you'd have time to gather everything for them."

Rachel had continued talking about what the CDC was going to do as they walked through the main doors and then toward the basement, where his office was located. Morris didn't care what the government did, as long as they left his research alone.

He sent Rachel to the copier with a stack of research as soon as they arrived at the lab, and he copied the work saved on his computer to flash drives. Sure, they could have his files, but he wasn't giving up on the study entirely, and no way was he just giving everything away. The migraine research took up a decade of his career. He might not be able to cure the patients infected with a parasite, but regular migraine sufferers still needed treatment.

What if every cluster headache was caused by a parasite? Maybe it's been here all along.

He silenced the voice in his head with a promise to explore that avenue later. Right now, he wanted to take advantage of the opportunity to work with the CDC's scientists. Being in on the ground floor of a parasite discovery would give him serious gas career-wise. He wasn't about to abandon ship because the feds were on the case.

Morris glanced at his watch. Twenty minutes left. He put the two flash drives containing his study files into an envelope and then tucked it into his pocket before the phone rang. Morris picked it up. "Yeah?"

"Hey," Rachel replied. "She's here."

"She's early."

"Yeah, you can tell her that."

He sighed. "Send her in."

On the desk was a box containing binders and more flash drives; copies of his files. Someone knocked on the door and then it opened. A tall figure wearing an orange suit walked in.

"Dr. Jenkins?" The voice was female. As she approached the desk, he saw her face through the plastic front of her hood. She smiled.

"Morris," he stood and held out his hand.

She grasped it in a firm shake and then stepped back. "I'm Catherine Fairchild."

"Have you had much time to look over the files at the hospital?" He didn't like that she wore the suit. That meant they thought the lab was contaminated. Possibly the entire university and hospital. Not good.

"For Dr. Foster's patient, Jennifer Carlton, yes," she said. "And I examined two men who arrived at the ER yesterday. One is deceased now."

"Oh," Morris said. "Same as Jenny?"

"No. Secondary infection, we think. He used a dirty knife when he tried to gouge his eyes out."

Morris shook his head. "I'd have called you before now, but we only just saw the pattern. Until I met Jenny, I believed these were just run-of-the-mill cluster headaches."

"So I heard," she pointed to the file box. "Is this for me?"

"Yes. It's all the work I've done on migraine clusters, although the only data that you'll find relevant is what I collected over the past six months or so."

"I'll look at all of it, just in case."

"Whatever you need."

"I'll have to take your computer as well."

Good thing he made copies for himself. "It's all in the files there."

"You may have missed something," she said.

"I've analyzed the data thoroughly—"

"I meant when you copied the files, you may have missed one. As for analysis, it never hurts to have someone new look at it. You never know what a set of fresh eyes will find, right?"

"Of course. If it helps, we are almost positive it's a parasite."

She smiled again. Christ, she was beautiful, even in the ridiculous suit. Rachel hadn't exaggerated.

"Why do you think that?" she asked.

"We found eggs in the brain tissue of a man who killed himself after suffering with the headaches for months. And then there's Jenny, whose brain exploded during surgery. We saw what looks like a worm in her scans, which leads me to believe it's a parasite of some kind. Perhaps one that feeds on brain tissue."

"No one told me you had samples. Not a single mention of eggs, actually."

"You'll find the lab's results in these files, as well as my hypotheses about the eggs."

"I'd prefer to see the samples myself."

"I wish I could give them to you, but they're gone."

"Where?"

"They disintegrated before we could run more tests."

"Oh. I suppose we could retrieve samples from the patient who died yesterday."

"The eggs deteriorate rapidly when exposed to air, so if there were any in Jenny's brain, they may have disappeared by now."

"Won't hurt to look anyway. We haven't run the autopsy on the other patient yet, so I'll figure out a way to examine his brain tissue without exposing it."

Morris tried not to smile. "You won't see the eggs unless you take samples. You can't take samples without opening the skull and removing tissue."

"As I said, I'll figure out a way. Did you get any data from the samples before they disappeared?"

"Nothing conclusive. Those reports are in the file. Maybe you'll see something I didn't."

"Maybe."

"I was thinking we should take soil samples from an excavation site a good portion of the patients worked on." Morris resisted the urge to massage his temples, where a dull ache had formed. "Actually, I believe my assistant was supposed to go there yesterday, but she may have been sidetracked by Jenny's death."

"It may give us some information."

"The site is the only link between all of the patients."

"That you've seen. I'm not ruling anything out."

Morris nodded. God, his fucking head was pounding. "What do you think is happening to these people?"

"I can't say."

"I mean," he pressed his nose. "Do you have any theories? I know it's early, but you must have some ideas."

"I'm leaning toward parasite as well. Until I get my hands on a live patient, though, who would have viable eggs in their brain, I assume, I can't begin to develop a suitable treatment. For now, we've quarantined anyone who worked with Doctor Foster's patient, as well as anyone who came in contact with her before she was admitted."

"She worked on the burial site I just men—"

"Your assistant filled us in. We're in the process of contacting and quarantining everyone who worked on that site and anyone who encountered them afterward. There are several police officers, forensic specialists, and construction workers we've yet to make contact with. After we've contacted everyone, we'll have to look into families and friends. The list will be very long, I imagine."

"Shit. That's extreme."

"Not when we could be looking at an epidemic, it's not. I'd prefer to be overly cautious and bring everyone in, even if that means I have to put a whole city in quarantine. We'll treat everyone with a broad spectrum antiparasitic. It'll probably be ineffective if this is a parasite we've never encountered, but it can't hurt to try. Those who've shown no symptoms after a week will be released."

"Sounds reasonable," he said. "But the man hours involved just in gathering information will be astronomical."

"The government can handle it. You realize we'll have to quarantine you and your staff, as well as this lab."

No, he didn't realize that. "Why?"

"Because not only have you worked with several of these patients, but you've also handled their biological material. From what I've learned since arriving, no one followed infectious diseases protocols when studying or treating these patients."

"But I'm fine," he said.

Except for the headaches.

"You're fine *now*. I'd rather keep you under observation for a while, so if symptoms appear, we can make an effort to treat them before it becomes a problem."

She meant before he killed himself or someone else. Morris wasn't prepared to leave his work. Quarantine meant he'd be stuck at home, or worse, in a hospital. If they made him leave now all he'd have is the flash drives in his pocket. He needed the files he told Rachel to hide in the utility room.

"Doctor Jenkins," she said.

"Call me Morris."

"All right. Morris, I know this is difficult. You've worked a long time on this study and you've made great strides in migraine treatment."

"Thanks."

"But these people aren't suffering from migraines. They're infected with a parasite. The eggs you found are a concern, as is the fact a woman's brain exploded when you tried to remove the parasite. The link you've found to the burial site could be what helps us identify and treat it, so you've done the critical part already. We're just here to connect the dots you've revealed. I will make sure you receive credit for all of your work up to this point, and for any help you're able to give down the road."

"I know. It's not about credit." Except it was. "I just hate to lose steam, you know?"

"Your files will be returned. I promise. And I don't see any reason we can't work together. I can quarantine you here, if that's preferable. We can set up a room that allows us to do that."

"I'm positive I'm not infected." Well, he hoped he wasn't.

"We're preparing an exam room for you right now," she said. "If we find nothing, you'll be free to participate in our investigation in a limited capacity."

"Limited?"

"Yes. But don't worry. As I said, I'll give you full credit for your work."

She left the room, leaving the door open. Morris took his cellphone from his pocket. Rachel would've left by now, he hoped. If they wouldn't let him leave, he could at least make sure he had someone on the outside.

He scrolled through his contacts, found Rachel's name, and then texted a short message.

"Get out of the hospital and stay away from the lab."

* * *

Catherine spent several hours reading Dr. Jenkins' notes. He had been meticulous in his documentation of each subject's symptoms and the results of treatment. Everything was by the book. Unbiased and scientific. Six months ago, though, he began keeping record of his own thoughts on several patients linked by the burial site. These ranged from wild theories to sound medical hypotheses, but most of the hastily scribbled notes were useless to her. He had no proof to support his theories, and the symptoms didn't make sense. Cluster migraines did not make people violent.

"Because they aren't migraines," she said and turned off the computer. "Looking under the wrong bush, Mr. Jenkins."

When the team returned with the soil samples, maybe she'd make some headway. The pressure of George and his goons breathing down her neck didn't help. He wanted to resolve the issue quickly and quietly, rather than take the time to study its origins and devise a safe treatment. "Just get rid of the problem before it becomes a crisis," he'd said.

She convinced him to hold off on the government sanctioned culling of infected people and the subsequent cover up, but he wouldn't stay away for long. He'd been clear he cared more about eliminating the threat against the population as a whole than saving the lives of the few already infected.

Her phone chimed. She shifted papers around the desk until she found it. "Catherine Fairchild."

"Hey," George replied "What've you got? Is it a virus or a parasite?"

Not even twenty-four hours and she already felt his breath on her neck. "I don't have much yet, but we just arrived. I told you I'd need at least a week to identify what we're dealing with."

"How many infected?"

"You know it's impossible to determine that without more information."

"Okay, how many dead?"

"Four confirmed, but that's over the course of a few months."

"Uh huh," he said. "And they're all linked to the burial site?"

"I think so."

"They are. I know it. We found the files."

"What files?"

He sighed. "I told you I recognized the address for that site. There's a history there. Lots of illness and death. Suicides and homicides mostly."

"So?"

"I can't discuss the particulars over the phone. Once I get you approved for a higher clearance, I'll stop by and we'll talk."

"Why would I need a higher—?"

"The information is classified, Catherine. I already told you that."

"If you already know what this is, telling me will only help, clearance or not."

"Let's just say we thought we dealt with that place a long time ago. I've got the go ahead to do what's necessary to resolve it finally."

"By resolve you mean..."

"You know what I mean."

She recalled his idea of "resolution" for a small tribe in Africa about five years ago. The tribe no longer existed. Catherine wasn't sure she wanted a higher clearance. Might be better not to know why he thought death would be a better alternative for these people.

"I think you're overreacting. If we eliminated every biological threat to humanity, we'd have no human race left."

"I know," George continued. "You have a thing about the preservation of life."

"That thing is called being a human being."

"We may not have the luxury of taking a moral high ground here. This thing you've stumbled on is far deadlier if we let it spread beyond those already infected."

"It'd be better to figure out treatment, so we can treat future infections and—"

"It won't come back when I'm done."

"You just said you dealt with it before. Obviously, it didn't work."

A sigh. "I did deal with it, but I didn't go far enough in the eradication measures. I used to be like you. I thought saving every life mattered, but sometimes you don't have the luxury of being humane. There are things out there that can't be cured or managed with medication. This threat is... I can't get into it right now, as I said before. Just know that it is not something we should take lightly. If my suspicions are correct, this is a national security matter, not just a health crisis."

"Just" a health crisis... she sighed. "Give me a week to confirm it's a parasite and not a virus. Can you do that?"

"How's the quarantine going?"

She loved how he just ignored her question. He should've been a politician. "We've got those who worked the site isolated in a secure wing at the hospital. We're using a home quarantine program for secondary contacts, and I'm hoping that's all we'll need."

"Nope."

"What do you mean, nope?"

"I mean, it's not enough. If this is what I think it is, you need to gather anyone who worked the site and anyone who has had any physical contact with those people. I'm talking even just brushing their shoulder in an elevator, if it's possible to get that information. Get them all in one place, preferably away from everyone else."

Now he was just being insane. "That's impossible. There were at least twenty people on that site. Factor in family, coworkers, friends... that many people would be noticed. We'll have panic if we try to get all of them to submit to quarantine."

"Once the death toll starts rising, panic will be an understatement."

"I can't just round people up and—"

"You can and you *must*. Look, if it becomes problematic, just make a statement to the media. Call it a viral outbreak and request that anyone showing symptoms check into the hospital immediately. If they think it's a matter of life or death, you'll have to beat them back with a stick. They'll be begging for your help."

"That's a lie, though. It's not the infection that's deadly."

"It can be."

"I won't exaggerate to scare people."

"Just a white lie. Convince them to come to the hospital willingly. I don't care what you say, as long as they consent to examination. You can quarantine them once they're in your care Nothing they can do about it. I can handle the rest."

"But if they don't come home—"

"We'll have a story ready for the public. In the meantime, I'm sending a team to help you gather them all up."

"You're not coming?" Maybe she could avoid his "final solution" long enough to develop a treatment.

"Not yet. I have an important matter I have to take care of. I'll join you later, though."

"I don't need a bunch of soldiers running around here causing panic."

"They'll be undercover. Medical staff. How's that?"

"Do I have a choice?"

"Not really."

Catherine rubbed her forehead. "Fine. But tell them I'm in charge."

"Sure, you are. We'll talk again in a couple of days."

Before she could object to his overseeing the project personally, George ended the call.

"Shit." Catherine set the phone on the desk and returned to Dr. Jenkins' notes. She'd read a couple of lines when the phone chimed again. "George, I said I—"

"Hey, boss," Jacob interrupted. "You close to the hospital?"

"I'm next door at the university. Why?"

"Suit up and get to the ER"

"What's happened?"

"Just get over here. Now."

CHAPTER 9

Rachel sat in her car puzzling over Morris's text when she saw the van stop in front of the hospital. Flu, he said, but damn if he wasn't acting like some of their research patients. The thought of Morris dying made her nauseous. True, he could be an asshole when it came to his research, and he wouldn't know flirting if someone whacked him in the face with it, but she liked him. She more than liked him. If he were sick, she couldn't leave him in there alone, without friends to look out for his best interests.

The van's side door opened and then people in white suits filed out. Rachel counted five. Another car pulled into the parking lot near the van. This one was black. She slouched down in her seat. The car door opened and Dr. Fairchild emerged. She too wore a suit, but she carried the helmet under her arm. She joined the occupants of the van, and after speaking to her companions, she put the helmet on her head. The person next to her secured it and then she nodded. Together, they walked toward the emergency room doors.

Rachel had to know what was happening. Maybe Maya was working today. She could get the details without speaking to Fairchild. Something about her bugged Rachel. Morris's weird text didn't help alleviate that feeling.

As she approached the emergency doors, three men in black suits walked toward her from the left side of the parking lot. She put her head down and walked faster. He'd told her to stay away. Would they force her to stay now? Could they do that?

They caught up quickly, but as she entered the lobby,

they walked past her and kept going toward the elevators at the end of the hall.

Rachel stopped at the desk. "Hey," she said to the girl behind the window. "Is Maya on today?"

"She's on five. Got quarantined."

"Shit, I forgot about that. Is she all right? Are they allowing visitors?"

The girl shrugged. "No visitors, medical staff or otherwise. She seemed okay to me, but then, I guess the dozen or so people they took up there yesterday looked fine too. They put this partition up. Said if I open it for any reason, I'll be up there too. Really weird shit going on. You should go, just in case. Try County instead if you really need a doctor, or better yet, go to your family doctor. Seriously."

"What do you mean?"

"CDC came in this morning, requested all records relating to headaches, and then rounded up every nurse, doctor and volunteer that got near any of those patients. Put them all on the fifth floor after clearing it out. They even called people at home. Said there was an emergency and then carted them off. We got enough trouble finding beds for sick patients, and they go forcing healthy people to take up an entire floor."

Rachel nodded. "Can I go up there?"

She laughed. "You can try. Heard they got a guard posted at every elevator. Took everyone's cell phones too. Anyone who contacts a headache patient without a suit is quarantined. Safety precaution, they said."

"Wow." What had Dr. Fairchild discovered?

"Yeah. Like I said, weird shit. Hey, if you do go up there," the woman said. "See if you can find Toby Brinson."

"Okay?" She didn't plan to ask around too much. Her mission was more of a reconnaissance thing. Talking to someone meant being discovered and she wasn't sure that was the best idea at the moment.

"He's my boyfriend," the girl said. "Paramedic. They

quarantined him last night. Just want to know he's okay."

Rachel nodded. "I'll see if anyone can tell me anything." She had to get up there, but she didn't want to deal with Fairchild's people. Maybe Morris meant she should stay away from them. Elevators were out, obviously. Maybe... she smiled. "Hey, are the doors to the stairs still unlocked?"

"Sure. Fire codes and all."

"Even the ones in the Kente wing?"

"They're doing construction over there."

"I know."

"Of course, the CDC stopped all that. Another dozen beds we can't fucking use. Pardon my French."

Rachel smiled. "Yeah, it's ridiculous. Thanks for your help. I really should go."

"Don't forget about Toby."

"I won't," Rachel lied.

She walked through the ER doors, past the waiting room, which was surprisingly quiet, and down the hallway toward the Kente Wing. They'd fundraised to update it for a few years. It was the only part of the hospital, apart from the basement, that remained of the original structure. Every other floor had been remodeled or completely demolished to make way for state-of-the-art additions.

Rachel pulled the yellow tape from the door, and then went inside. Plastic sheets hung from the ceiling to contain construction debris. In the dim light, these cast shadows that moved with the air pumping in through the vents. A couple of times, she thought she saw someone following her. Just shadows, she told herself. As she approached the stairwell, she looked behind her to confirm she was alone.

Taking a deep breath, Rachel opened the door and then started up the stairs. They'd killed the power to the stairwell, so it was almost entirely dark, except for a square of light shining from the doors leading to each floor as she passed.

Finally, Rachel approached the fifth-floor landing. She peeked through small glass window in the door. Nothing.

Carefully, she pressed the latch down and then pulled the door open. It creaked, but no alarm sounded. Her heart pounded. God, this was silly. Why should she fear Dr. Fairchild's team? They were there to help.

Still, the tightness in her belly warned her to avoid detection. Morris would laugh at her amateur sleuthing. Maybe. If he was still alive. She hoped he wasn't infected.

A few steps into the hallway, she paused. No one guarded the doors. In fact, no one seemed to be there at all, which was odd. If the floor was full of patients, there should be nurses. A doctor at least. If they were quarantined, as the nurse said, then someone should be keeping an eye on the doors, making sure no one got on the floor.

A crash startled her. Shouts, and then a scream. Rachel pressed herself against the wall as she walked toward the noise. She searched for potential exits, just in case. Had to make it to the other end of the hallway to reach the other door to the stairs. Not good.

A white suited figure ran down the hallway toward her. She held her breath, looked at the floor, prayed they didn't ask her for identification, but the person ran into a room three doors down. Rachel turned to follow and then slid quietly into the room next to it.

She heard several people talking excitedly. More screaming and then nothing. Footsteps followed.

"These people must be moved," Dr. Fairchild said. "I want them all in the ward we set up at the university by this evening."

She saw shadows through the narrow pane of glass in the door. They must be right outside the room. Rachel pressed her back against the wall. She couldn't leave without revealing herself.

"You're joking, right?" a man said. "There's at least two dozen people here."

"If we leave them, we risk contaminating the entire hospital."

"University labs seem like the bigger risk. It's a school full of staff and students."

"The semester is almost finished. Students will be leaving for the summer."

"But still, all of the researchers and staff..."

Dr. Fairchild said nothing.

"I mean," the man continued, "As long as the rooms are locked, this is way more—"

"We have a building full of patients, visitors, doctors, nurses and other staff. One mistake, one rogue patient getting past our perimeter, and the entire place is compromised. That means hundreds, rather than dozens of people infected. I'd rather not give that many people a death sentence."

"The parasite doesn't kill—"

"It doesn't matter. We're trying to contain the illness, not spread it. The labs at the university are contained. I've set up *proper* isolation units. Only authorized personnel with keycards can get in or out. Anyone can get in here. Look at all the access points. Move them to the other ward. It's got one entry point. Once they're all in, lock the fire escapes and quarantine the entire building."

"Even the students?"

"No," Dr. Fairchild said and then paused. "We'll evacuate the staff and students who aren't part of Dr. Jenkins's research, and then we'll close the entire school."

"People will panic."

"We'll say there was an accident in the labs. No one will ask questions, because there's a protocol in place that includes a lockdown. Then, lock all of the patients in their rooms with a guard on every door."

"We don't have enough people for that."

"So, one guard for every two or three. I don't know. Figure it out. Just make sure we have eyes on all patients at all times. I want to avoid another situation like this. I should have more people here to help by morning. When they arrive, we'll post someone at reception in the main lobby too. I'll see about getting some cameras installed, so we can observe from a single station, but we won't hold our breath on that. Tell everyone that no one without proper identification gets in or out. Clear?"

Rachel didn't realize it was that contagious. Sure, if you have contact, the parasite might pass from one to another, but just being in the same area couldn't be dangerous. If it was... she didn't want to finish the thought.

"Just seems extreme. It's not airborne," the man said.

"That may have changed."

"It hasn't changed."

"We lost three tonight," Dr. Fairchild said. "And they weren't even symptomatic until a few hours ago. One of the nurses is infected, and she's only worked at the desk. Never had contact with a patient."

"So she says."

A sigh. "Let's err on the side of caution and believe she's being honest. It could be airborne. You want to risk an entire hospital full of people getting sick?"

"No."

"Then get them ready for transport to the university's lab. It's not far. Take them in the loading doors at the back. I'll get a team ready to receive. Tell Michelle to speak to the school officials and begin closing it down. I'll need to examine any students or staff working in the labs during the last six months as well."

"Okay, but what about the quarantine program? We haven't rounded everyone up yet. Not sure how we can guard rooms and do the door-to-door, unless we clone ourselves."

"We're coordinating with the NSA from here on out, so we'll have lots of people very soon."

"Is it true they want to euthanize?"

Rachel covered her mouth.

"Who told you that?"

"I just heard—"

"Don't indulge rumors. I hear that again, from anyone, and they'll be fired. Understood."

"Yes."

"And don't worry about the quarantine program. I'm holding a press conference soon. They'll come in on their own after that."

"What are you going to say?"

A sigh. "It's not important. Just do your job."

"Yes, ma'am."

"God, stop calling me that. Dr. Fairchild will do."

Footsteps again. The ding of the elevator. Rachel waited, breath held, until she heard nothing else. Dr. Fairchild didn't answer his question. She didn't say yes, they were euthanizing, but she didn't say no either.

* * *

George's team arrived the next morning. Catherine had little time to prepare her own people, so when they showed up dressed in combat boots and tactical gear, some panic ensued. She entered the lobby of the university's research department to a cacophony of shouts and, unfortunately, guns.

"Could I have everyone's attention please?" she shouted over the ruckus.

Slowly, but not immediately, the din died down. She waited until most of them looked at her before she spoke again. "I would appreciate it if you put the guns away."

The five or six men guilty of brandishing their weapons obeyed, although they glared at Catherine's colleagues as they did so.

"My name is Catherine Fairchild. I understand that you have orders to assist us, but while you are here, I am in charge. Is that clear?"

Several nods.

"Good. Now, we are dealing with an extremely

dangerous illness. We are not fighting a war." She noticed several of her people glare at George's team as she spoke. "And because people will panic, as is common in situations like this because they're scared, we need a bit of muscle to prevent a riot. However, I don't want violence." She tried to meet everyone's gaze as she spoke. "From anyone. Clear?"

Nods. A few murmured "Yes, ma'am."

"In order to accomplish our goal of containment and treatment, we have to work together. To safely quarantine the patients and avoid infecting ourselves, we need to be cautious. At the moment, I'm not entirely sure how the parasite is passed from one host to the next, so you must always wear protective gear when dealing with patients to avoid infection."

"Ma'am," a tall man dressed in a black suit said. "Our orders are to eliminate the threat. We weren't informed about a quarantine. It's going to be pretty hard to deal with resistance if we have to wear those space suits."

"Those space suits will ensure you don't become part of the threat you're supposed to eliminate." She knew she couldn't trust George, but foolishly hoped he'd keep his word about letting her deal with this her way. "And to be clear, we're only identifying potential illness and containing it. No elimination."

"I have my orders."

"And now you have new ones."

"With respect, you're not my superior."

"But I am in charge of this project. You will follow my orders or you can leave."

"I won't walk out on a mission, ma'am. Just telling you what my orders are."

"Well, your boss should be here very soon, so you can take that up with him when he arrives. My agreement with him was to collect and detain potential hosts. No violence and definitely no elimination."

"If these so-called hosts resist containment?"

"If they resist," Catherine said. "You will sedate them, but only if there is no other option. I do not want anyone harmed. That only causes panic. We want the public to believe patients are coming in willingly to avoid unnecessary chaos. Clear?"

"Yes, ma'am."

"Good." Catherine opened the folder she held. "I have a list of names and addresses here. At the moment, there are forty-seven, but I expect that number to grow the longer we take to round them up. We also need a team to remain here to monitor the isolation units. Patients can and have become violent and suicidal, so we can't leave them unattended."

"How many units?" the man asked.

"We've set up six rooms with four patients in each. I should have twelve more ready by morning."

"I can leave six behind to guard the doors, but they have no medical training. We'd be more useful in the field."

She'd rather keep them all at the university, away from the public, but he was right. If anyone resisted quarantine, George's team would know how to handle the situation. "I think it'd be wise to divide into several teams consisting of both medical personnel and... law enforcement. One team will remain here, the rest will work their way through the list. Who is the senior member of your team?"

The man she'd been speaking to raised his hand. "I'm team leader, ma'am."

"First, stop calling me ma'am. Catherine or Dr. Fairchild will do."

"Yes, m—Dr. Fairchild. You can call me Tom."

"Tom, I'll let you decide how many teams are required and divide our people accordingly."

"Understood."

"I want at least two of my people with each team. They can advise you on the protocol you must follow to avoid infection." She eyed the team dressed in black shirts, pants, boots and hats. They'd stand out like sore thumbs. Catherine sighed. "And we need to go in as medical personnel to avoid arousing suspicion, so everyone must change into scrubs."

George's people grumbled at this, but no one refused.

"David?" she turned and David, a lab assistant, stepped forward. "I need you to run over to the hospital to fetch enough scrubs for everyone."

"Where would I find those?"

"In the laundry room. Basement, I think. There should be freshly laundered ones either in the laundry or nearby. Do *not* take any from the floors."

"What if I just grab whatever I can find, bring them here and then we wash them ourselves? That way we know they're not contaminated."

"Good idea. Wear your suit when you go in, just to be safe."

"When you arrive at an address," Catherine continued as David left the lobby. "You will explain there is a medical emergency and ask the patient to come with you. If the patient refuses, then you may sedate them. I prefer that medical personnel handle the drugs, if that's all right with you."

Tom nodded.

"Thank you." Catherine took a breath. "When you go to these homes, it's probably best to use vehicles that won't raise any questions, so black vans or whatever it is you're used to using aren't the best option."

"What are we going to use then?" Tom asked. "Can't transport them all in cars."

"I'll contact the hospital and see if we can get an ambulance to accompany each team. If someone approaches you, the answers you give are simple; you are responding to a medical emergency. Ask the subject to stay back, as the patient in your care is highly contagious. That is all you say."

"That won't cause panic?"

"Less panic than armed men storming a home and forcefully removing the occupant and shoving them in an unmarked van. Definitely less panic than giving no answers at all."

"Understood."

Catherine smiled. "Good. Now, once the patient is removed from the home, you will seal the home, and someone should stay behind to make sure no one goes in until a research team arrives to process the scene. Oh, and no one goes inside a home without protective gear. Understood?"

Everyone nodded.

"Again," Tom interrupted. "Won't guards and caution tape cause panic?"

"I trust you to figure out a way to blend in."

He scowled.

"For those of you who haven't witnessed this parasite's effects," Catherine continued. "I can't stress enough the seriousness of the situation. If you are exposed, you will be quarantined with the people you're collecting. Follow every protocol my people provide, and do not be careless."

"Is it deadly?" someone asked. "I heard it just causes headaches and flu symptoms."

Oh, the wonderfully inaccurate ways of the rumor mill. Catherine shook her head. "It's not deadly on its own. However, if the NSA's people have their way, infection will most assuredly result in death."

Tom smiled. "Understood."

* * *

When they came for him, Bob didn't panic. His wife had suffered from migraine headaches for three months. She even took sick leave from work, which was unusual for her. In all the years Ginny had worked as a lab technician, she'd only taken time off when their son went away to college. Said she needed a day of mourning.

At first, he thought maybe she had some kind of monster

flu, but her personality changed too. Always a gentle soul, Ginny suddenly sprinkled profanities over every sentence. Her temper fired quickly, and she said terrible things to him when he attempted to help her. Worse than that, over the past few weeks, she'd become so depressed, he couldn't even convince her to get in the shower. She just laid in bed, curtains drawn, eyes closed.

They'd admitted her to the hospital after she'd downed an entire bottle of pain killers. She seemed peaceful now, but the doctors said the headaches still troubled her. They said the cause could be environmental. Something in the house might be making her sick. He figured the men in white suits were sent by the hospital to inspect their home to find a cause for Ginny's suffering.

Then they asked him to go with them. He'd gone, but as they drove away, he saw more white suits sealing his front door with yellow tape. A couple of them stayed outside, near a black SUV, almost like they were guarding the house.

Still, he didn't panic. He saved that for the hospital, after they locked him in a room with another guy who looked almost as bewildered as Bob felt.

"Why are we here?" Bob asked the guy.

"Dunno," the guy said. "Said something about a virus."

"A what?"

The guy shrugged.

"I'm Bob, by the way," he walked to the man's bed.

"Leo," he said, but didn't take Bob's outstretched hand.

Bob walked back to the bed on the opposite side of the room and then sat. His head hurt. Stress always made him ill. Rubbing his temples, he went over the past few days. Nothing out of the ordinary had happened, except for his wife's illness. Maybe they found out she had something contagious, like meningitis. Was that contagious enough to warrant forced quarantine?

"Hey, would they quarantine us for meningitis?"

Leo shook his head. "I don't think so. My brother died

from that when we were kids. They'd treat us with antibiotics if it's bacterial. Actually, I'm not sure what they'd do for a viral case. I'm sure they have drugs for that too."

Bob's head pounded now. He had to pause before speaking again just to catch his breath. He could have whatever Ginny had. If it was meningitis, how long before it became lethal? Was Ginny still alive? He never thought to ask. Never considered she might not be okay.

"You know someone who was sick?" Leo asked.

"My wife had headaches for days. Meningitis can do that, I think. I wondered if maybe that's what she had, so they brought me in so I don't spread it around."

"Headaches?" Leo, who formerly seemed like he didn't give a damn about Bob's situation, sat up in his bead. "Migraines?"

"Yeah. She's been off work, which isn't like her. Started acting strange too and then she had an accident, so I had to call an ambulance."

"Suicidal?"

He shrugged. "I wouldn't say that." She took the pills accidentally. Just lost track of the number, he'd told himself. Except, she had mentioned something about not wanting to exist anymore. Did that make her suicidal? Bob didn't see it that way at the time, but now...

"Funny you mention headaches, though," Leo said. "A couple of days ago, I was on the subway when this guy just completely lost his mind. Said something about fire in his head. After he attacked some people, he tried to gouge his eyes out. Someone tried to restrain him, and he fell, but when he went down, he hit his head. He wasn't breathing, though, and no one tried to help him, so I—"

"You gave him CPR."

"Yeah, until the cops and an ambulance came. I thought maybe he was on some kind of drug or whatever, that fucked with his brain. God knows what kind of shit junkies are carrying around, so I got checked out at the hospital just in case. They told me I had nothing to worry about, because the guy was mentally unstable, not high or sick, but then these men showed up at my house last night, saying I had to go with them."

"Never said why?"

"Just said the doctor would explain it all. So far, no one's explained shit."

The pain in Bob's head sharpened, settling behind his eyes. He lay down, but it didn't help. Someone knocked on the door. While he knew it couldn't be that loud, the sound ricocheted around his brain.

"Good morning, gentlemen," a woman said. Bob didn't sit up. "Mr. Giles, are you not feeling well?"

Bob shook his head. "Just wondering why I'm here."

"Me too," Leo said. "Are you the doctor?"

"I'm Doctor Fairchild," she confirmed. "First, I'd like to examine each of you, and then we'll talk about what's going on. Is that okay?"

"Guess we don't have much choice," Leo said. "What's with the suit?"

Bob opened his eyes. Dr. Fairchild stood next to his bed. She wore a white suit, like the men who'd picked him up earlier wore. "This isn't a good sign."

"Mr. Giles," she said as she shone a light into his eyes, causing the pain to skyrocket from annoying to unbearable, "your wife was admitted recently complaining of migraine headaches."

"Yeah, but she's okay, right?"

She nodded. "At the moment, she's sedated and stable."

"At the—"

"We believe there is a parasite infecting her brain," she continued. "Until we can isolate and treat it, we decided it's best to quarantine anyone showing symptoms so that we can keep it contained."

"Uh," Leo said. "I don't have symptoms."

Dr. Fairchild put a strange device on Bob's forehead.

Thermometer, he told himself.

"The incubation period is often brief," she said to Leo. "So, I believe that if you are infected, you will exhibit symptoms very soon. I'd rather have you here, where we can monitor you, rather than out there, where you could pass it on to others or harm yourself."

Bob had no words. Even if he did, his thoughts had jumbled so thoroughly, he probably couldn't voice them. The thought of pushing words over his tongue exhausted him.

Dr. Fairchild walked to the end of the bed and then pulled the clipboard from the plastic pocket attached to the footboard. She opened it, wrote something inside, and then set it back in the pocket. "You told the nurse you've had headaches for a couple of days?"

Bob nodded. "Not migraines. Stress."

"Are you experiencing pain now?"

He closed his eyes, but the strange lights flickering just at the edges of his vision didn't go away. Instead, they seemed brighter.

"Mr. Giles?"

"Is this parasite deadly?" Leo asked, preventing Bob from responding.

"Not on its own," Dr. Fairchild said. "The virus causes cluster migraines, which can be excruciating. They often affect mood and emotional well-being, so patients can become depressed, suicidal, or, as you witnessed on the subway, they can become unusually aggressive. Not themselves."

Leo nodded. "How is the subway guy, by the way?"

"Dead."

"Oh."

"The virus didn't kill him," she said, as though that made it better. "He lost too much blood by the time they got him here. A secondary infection set in, worsening his condition. His heart stopped during the night and we were unable to revive him."

"I see."

Well Bob didn't see. They had to tell people. He would, but he couldn't speak.

"Mr. Giles," Dr. Fairchild's voice had softened. "I'm going to send a nurse in with something to help your pain."

"*Ungh*," Bob managed.

"And then we'll take you upstairs for some tests."

Bob said nothing. Get on with the painkillers. That's all he needed. Then he'd be right as rain. Not that rain was right. That saying was stupid. Everyone was stupid. He just wanted drugs. All the drugs.

"Mr. Giles?"

"Yeah?"

"Can you see me?"

Bob didn't realize he'd opened his eyes. He saw lights and colors, but nothing defined. No edges. "No."

"Okay," she pressed the neck of her suit. "Could I have some help in 3B, please?"

"What?" he asked, although the sound he heard coming from his mouth sounded odd. A language he didn't understand.

"Don't worry, Mr. Giles. We're going to help you."

Help. Good. Bob closed his eyes again. The lights were gone. The pain had moved to the back of his head and dulled to a breathtaking hum. He breathed through his mouth, which seemed to make it better. Something about the air passing through his nose made his brain angry.

Angry brains. Angry birds. Stupid game. He played it all the time at work. Terrible at it. Still played. Probably had a sub—*sss*... the word escaped him. Didn't matter.

"Drugs," he said in his new, strange language. "Please."

"Okay," Dr. Fairchild said somewhere far away. Something touched his face... A mask? "We're taking you upstairs now."

Bob felt the bed floating. Words spoken, but he didn't understand. Something pinched his hand, and then clouds formed at the edges of his mind. The clouds were nice. They softened the fire's fury. Made the pain bearable.

* * *

"Is this what you saw?" Catherine pointed to the image.

Morris leaned forward. It was difficult to see the image through the glass barrier, but the shadow was unmistakable. "Yes. That's the parasite."

"Interesting." Catherine put another image against the window. "This was taken about ten seconds after the first."

The shadow, an elongated oval shape, had changed position in the second image. "It can't..."

"Can't what?"

"Move that fast. I mean, do you know what that implies?"

She nodded. "Nothing good. I wondered if perhaps it's not that it moved, but that there are more than one."

"You mean, they're reproducing in the host?"

She nodded. "If they feed off the host, it stands to reason they'd reproduce as well. You did find eggs, right?"

"Yes."

"So that answers your question. Some patients exhibit extremely intense symptoms, while others do not. I'm hypothesizing that those infected with multiple parasites are the ones becoming aggressive or suicidal."

"Whose scans are these?" Morris waited for the answer he dreaded hearing.

"New patient," she said.

He released the air in his lungs. Not his brain. Thank God. "Is he or she dead?"

"No, he's early stages. His wife contracted the parasite first, and we picked him up as a precaution. Good thing we did. Within hours of admitting him, he developed symptoms. Now he's sedated, but he has a bad heart, and the stress caused by the headaches is creating complications."

Not good. Morris stared at the image. If it could move from the front of the brain to the back in ten seconds, how could they possibly isolate and remove one to study it? "Any cases since yesterday?"

"Three."

He sighed. "From the patients you gathered?"

"Two are patients we put in isolation, and one walked into the ER late yesterday. She suffered a stroke this morning and died."

"Maybe you'll find it in her brain during autopsy."

"I found eggs. No parasite."

"You've done the autopsy already?"

"I began as soon as we called it. No time to waste, right?"

"I guess so."

"You said the eggs deteriorate rapidly, so I thought testing and documenting them as soon as possible was the wisest course of action."

"No, you're right. You're absolutely right. It's just overwhelming."

She smiled as she tucked the images into the large envelope she held. "I wish I had more news, but I've never seen anything like this. The eggs resemble nothing we've seen before and the biological material they leave behind hasn't been easy to identify. We're still running tests, of course."

"Which means?"

"I think this parasite is new."

Which meant they had no idea how it behaved or how to kill it before it killed its hosts. He tried not to let despair take over, but it clung to his chest no matter how hard he tried to shake it away. The headache returned while he waited for breakfast, and it rapidly intensified. He didn't tell Catherine, of course. She might sedate him and then he'd have no input into his own care.

"Still think quarantining everyone even remotely connected to that dig site is overkill?" she asked.

"No." Morris leaned his head against the window. The

cold glass felt nice. "I think it probably won't be enough."

CHAPTER 10

George arrived as Catherine finished her rounds. The teams had picked up half of the people on her list. Of that half, eleven showed symptoms of infection. Four of those were critical and had attempted self-harm. She spent most of the morning giving vague answers as to the cause of their suffering and the reasons for their quarantine.

When she arrived in the office she'd taken over to go over the test results she'd just received from the lab, she found George seated at the desk reading her files.

"Make yourself at home," she said, closing the door behind her.

"I have." George closed the file. "This is bad, Catherine. Really bad. Why do you have a patient in the room next door? Shouldn't he be in quarantine with the rest?"

"He's the one who found the pathogen, and as such, may have crucial information regarding finding an effective treatment, so I'd like to keep him close. The room is properly sealed and we've taken precautions."

"He can't be here."

"If we move him, we risk contaminating the entire lab."

"How do you know it's not already contaminated?"

"Protocols were followed. This isn't my first rodeo, as they say. The door is locked. He is in an isolation tent. Only I or select members of my team can gain entry to the room, and we wear the proper gear. Everything and everyone is properly decontaminated before exiting."

"Is he infected?"

"I'm not sure. Probably. Although his tests show no signs of infection, he's exhibiting all of the symptoms we've seen in infected patients."

"Wonderful."

"We're making headway. I isolated samples from a host's brain. While foreign organic material I found disintegrated rapidly, I was able to run a few tests on it."

"And?"

She held up the folder. "I haven't looked yet. May I?" she pointed to the laptop next to his elbow."

"Of course." George stood and then walked around the desk.

Catherine took his place. She opened the laptop, typed her password and then waited for the home screen to appear. She clicked the email icon, and then scrolled down until she found the one from the lab, which would contain images and more detailed results than the pages in her file.

She stared at the images, noting the time they were taken. The biological material they'd recovered lasted just under an hour before it disappeared. That wasn't the part that concerned her, though. It didn't match anything in the database. Human, animal, or otherwise. Nothing.

This couldn't be right. There had to be something with similar DNA. Without looking at George, lest she give away her distress, Catherine opened the folder. The comments made by her analysts echoed what she concluded based on the images. It had to be a mistake. Someone must've contaminated the sample or an algorithm had a glitch.

"Problem?" George asked.

"These results are useless. They don't make sense."

"Well, let me tell you a story, and then it might."

She glanced at him. "What?"

"You've been given clearance, so I'm going to tell you what your parasite is, and why we can't allow its hosts to live."

She closed the file. "Go on."

"A couple hundred years ago, people reported seeing

strange lights in the sky over the Baker Plantation," he said. "That's the site where those bones were found."

Catherine said nothing. She already knew this from Morris's research.

"There were a number of theories as to what they were and where they came from, but the bountiful harvest the following year ended the speculation. The residents decided the lights must be from God and that the Bakers' were blessed."

"That's ridiculous."

George smiled. "Soon after the harvest, residents of the plantation started experiencing headaches. These headaches were mind-altering in their severity. Eventually, the infected became depressed, suicidal... homicidal."

"As my patients are."

"Yes. At the time, the idea of anything other than something of this earth being the cause was unheard of. At most, they believed Satan had cursed them, or that God had forsaken them. They never imagined anything might exist beyond the heavens."

"You're talking about aliens?"

"Please, try not to interrupt."

She sighed. George did like his own voice. She waved her hand so he'd proceed with his story.

"To end their curse, the townsfolk locked the family and their servants inside the home and they burned it all to the ground."

"Jesus."

"Yes, a little extreme, but it did stop the infection."

"I will not kill people."

"Yet," George said. "After the fire, a relative took over the property, rebuilt and everything was fine for a year or two. But then the headaches returned."

"If they burned everything, then it wasn't a parasite."

He nodded. "The headaches returned after the new owner dug up the soil in the location where the lights were seen to begin planting a new crop. Again, no one knew what the cause was. The man killed himself and his servants. Luckily, he had no family to take with him."

"So, you're saying this is the same pathogen?"

"Let me finish."

Catherine checked her watch. "I have patients."

"The land passed through many hands, and the suicides and violent behavior continued with each new owner. It sat vacant for a time, and then, finally, in the late 1970's, the government realized there was more to it than just bad luck. We investigated, tested the soil, and the bodies, and then, when one of the investigators fell ill, we found biological material we couldn't explain."

"Like I've found now."

"Yes. Except, the results are not impossible or wrong. Your problem is extraterrestrial."

Catherine laughed. "You're joking."

"I wish."

"So, you're telling me that a spaceship landed and infected the soil?"

"There was nothing recovered from the site. No craft. No meteor rocks. Nothing."

"Then what was it?"

"We're not sure. We know *something* crashed on that site, and it left behind material that shouldn't be here. It probably wasn't intentional. Nothing but charred soil and vegetation was found, but it could've been a meteor, or an aircraft. Perhaps an investigative vessel simply doing research. Some of its research, we hypothesize, included the organisms infecting your patients now. They live in organic material such as soil, or the human body. Can't be killed by fire, obviously, so we believe the only way to eliminate them is to remove their food source."

"Which means kill anyone who might be infected."

"As they seem to rely on the host's brain to survive and reproduce, yes. There's no other option. Then we must cremate the bodies and then bury the ashes in a sealed container as deep as possible."

"Extreme."

"Necessary."

"What about the burial site? As long as that soil is accessible, people will continue to become infected."

"Already taken care of."

"How?"

"That property now belongs to the Federal government. We've started pouring concrete. By this time next week, the community will have a parking lot that serves the needs of almost all of the downtown businesses."

"Rather large for a parking lot."

"If we build a structure, they'll have to run water and sewer lines in the soil. Can't risk it."

She rubbed her eyes. "I still don't see the need for killing anyone. We may be able to treat them. Surgery could—"

"This isn't some bacteria or virus you can cure, Catherine. It is a parasite. A living creature that has defense mechanisms. If you try to remove the parasite, it causes the brain to swell."

She stared.

"Yes, I read the files and it's not the first time I've seen that happen. We can't risk any more casualties. It *must* be contained."

"We're trying."

"This isn't the CDC's show anymore, my dear." He smiled as though trying to soften the blow of his words. "It's a matter of national security, which reminds me, I've cancelled your press conference. No need for it now that we're involved."

"But I could find a cure."

"You won't, but you may study the parasite and your patients while we locate the remaining hosts. Once we have them all, though, I'm afraid my orders are quite clear and non-negotiable."

"But—"

"We must terminate the threat," he said. "Don't worry. I'll deal with the cover up, as usual. You just worry about keeping the patients comfortable until it's time to deal with them."

* * *

Morris heard voices. It took him a while to realize they came from his office next door. The one Catherine usurped. He sat up in his bed. The tent they'd placed him in obscured everything outside, but he knew they'd set up a perimeter around it, and then a decontamination chamber by the door.

The headache had subsided enough for his mind to clear.

"Yes, I read the files," a man's voice said. "We can't risk any more casualties. It must be contained."

"We're trying," Catherine replied.

"This isn't the CDC's show anymore, my dear. It's a matter of national security."

What did that mean?

"You may study the parasite and your patients while we locate any remaining hosts. Once we have them all, though, I'm afraid my orders are quite clear and non-negotiable."

"But—"

"We must terminate the threat," he said. "Don't worry. I'll deal with the cover up, as usual. You just worry about keeping the patients comfortable until it's time to deal with them."

Morris knew what that meant. Who was the man, though? Couldn't be from the CDC. They weren't in the business of killing sick people. Government? NSA maybe. He pressed his forehead. If they were rounding up potential hosts to the pathogen, then everyone who'd worked with him would be in quarantine.

And they'd all be dead soon.

Rachel...

Morris glanced at the small desk next to his bed. They hadn't removed much from the room, which served as a workspace and an extra room to store files and equipment. When he'd cleared the desk the month before to study his research without interruptions, he decided to keep the old phone he'd found. He opened the bottom drawer. Still there.

The phone was heavy; a relic from the nineties, he'd guess. The university never threw anything out. He wasn't even sure if it'd still work.

Standing took some effort. Christ, he felt so weak, but managed to get out of bed, and then, phone in hand, he crawled along the floor until he found a jack. The headache returned full force as he tried to insert the plug into the tiny hole. He tried several times before successfully plugging the phone into the jack beside the bed, and then he lifted the receiver.

Dial tone. Thank fucking God.

He held his hand over the keypad. Christ. He couldn't recall Rachel's number.

Morris breathed slowly. Relax. He closed his eyes. Numbers were his gift. He could recall anything relating to numbers, even if he'd only seen them briefly. He let his brain do the work and then, finally, he remembered.

As he dialed, Morris kept an eye on the dark blob on the right side of his tent. If it turned white, it meant someone had opened the door.

Ringing.

Rachel normally worked from home on Fridays, transcribing for Morris, because classes took up a considerable amount of time the first part of her week. He prayed she stuck to her schedule and didn't return to the lab.

"Hello?"

"Rachel?"

"Mo! Are you okay? Where are you? I went to the university, but I can't even get into the lab's parking lot. I've been calling you all night."

"I'm..." Sparks ignited over his eyes. Morris took a breath, waited for them to lose their fury and then licked his lips. "I'm in quarantine."

"Oh no."

"It's okay. I'm fine. Where are you?"

"I went to the hospital the other day. Snuck on to the quarantine ward. It's not good, Mo."

"Did they see you?"

"No. I got out of there fast. They're kind of losing their shit. Rounding up anyone who even thought about being infected."

"I know."

"I feel fine, but I doubt they'd listen, so I stayed at a friend's house last night. I'm coming back, though. Got my car out of the shop. Don't worry. I won't leave you there."

"No."

"No?"

"Don't come back."

"Mo—"

"Do not," he paused. Words made it to his throat, but his mouth refused to process them. *Fucksakes, this was annoying.* "Listen."

"Okay."

He waited for the headache to wrap around his head. It did this often. Once it circled his whole head, it migrated to the back of his neck, and then the pain ebbed somewhat, so he could think. "Heard them. Killing everyone."

"What? The parasite is killing everyone?"

"No. Well, yes. Not that, though. They're talking euthanization, Rachel."

"Dr. Fairchild said that was just rumor. They can't just—"

"Rachel," he said. "Just listen."

She said nothing, but he imagined her nodding.

"You have to run. Far as you can. Canada is good."

"Okay, now *you're* being ridiculous."

"If they find you, they'll bring you back and they'll kill you. Killing everyone exposed."

"They can't."

"They. Are."

"Fuck, Mo," Rachel whispered. "This is America. Free country and all that."

"Run, Rachel. Get rid of your phone." Lights danced in front of his vision. Morris resisted the urge to cry. He wouldn't let it beat him. Wouldn't become one of those lunatics stabbing himself in the face or curling up and just dying instead of dealing with the pain.

"You still there, Mo?"

"Yes. Just... get rid of your phone. Can track it. Buy a burner."

"This is some seriously secret agent shit. I can't go to Canada! I mean, honestly."

"Just go... somewhere. Christ... trying to save your life."

"This is crazy."

"When you're safe, find someone you trust."

"Oh, sure."

"And tell them everything. Saved files to the cloud. Password..."

"I know your password," she said. "But there's nothing in our files to support your mass killing story."

"Just do it. Okay?" The black blob outside his tent turned white. "Gotta go. Run. Please."

He hung up the phone and then slid it under the bed. As the whiteness disappeared, he laid on the floor.

"Morris?" Catherine said outside the tent. "Oh dear. Hello? I need some assistance in here. Full suit."

Morris slowly pushed himself up. "I'm okay."

"You are not."

He searched the floor for a weapon. Nothing, of course, except the now out of reach phone. Later. After she left. He'd leave his plastic prison and find a way to escape.

"Hold on," she said. "I've got something for the pain."

He heard a zipper and then plastic. Then the zipper again. Hands on his arms. He let her lift him and then guide him to the bed. The energy expended to call Rachel was more than he had in his reserves. He didn't fight the medication she gave him. Needed the rest.

Once he felt well enough again, he'd leave, and he'd tell the world what they were doing.

CHAPTER 11

After Morris ended the call, Rachel remained in her car on the side of the road and considered her options. If she'd been exposed to the parasite, she would need medical attention, but if Morris were right, going to the hospital would get her killed.

On the other hand, infection might kill her if she didn't seek help. Or it could make her kill someone else. Maybe she wasn't exposed. Could be fine. She had no headaches yet.

Cars sped past. The shoulder of a highway was a bad place to sit and contemplate one's fate. Rachel sighed and turned the key in the ignition. She waited for an extensive line of cars to pass and then merged into traffic. As she turned onto her exit, she decided to drive as far as she could and then maybe check into a motel for a few days. She'd find a shithole, where names weren't necessary and just wait.

Wait for what?

Morris? Death?

She passed the coffee shop where she and Morris stopped almost every morning to grab a latte for herself and a black, one sugar for him. The urge to cry hit her hard. Rachel swallowed, took a breath, and then counted to ten. Panicking wouldn't help.

As she neared her apartment, Rachel saw an ambulance in the parking lot. Near the main doors, two men in black suits stood. One talked on a cell phone, the other surveyed the road. Rachel kept driving. Morris wasn't exaggerating. Well, maybe he was about the killing, but not about them forcing everyone who might've been exposed into quarantine.

She led a pretty sheltered existence and she knew it. Her life had been easy and predictable. Graduate high school, break up with the boyfriend, because who needs the past when you're looking at the future, and go to college. Work under someone brilliant, maybe spark a relationship with an older professor. Once she made her professor fall in love with her, she'd become a renowned scientist under his brilliant tutelage, publish some papers, marry, have a kid or two, and then retire young, so she could author a book about her accomplishments.

It'd gone according to plan until today. Except for the affair with a brilliant professor. Morris was oblivious to anything but his work. Maybe he noticed and just wasn't interested. She preferred to think the former. Still, she'd done well, and had been happy with her life so far.

Now... Her skillset didn't extend to cloak and dagger shit or running for her life.

She drove toward the interstate but didn't take the exit. Instead, she pulled into a strip mall parking lot. Throw away her phone. Buy a burner. Baby steps.

Once she found a safe place to hide, she'd make a plan. One that didn't involve abandoning Morris to the feds or whoever had taken over the lab.

People had to know what was happening.

* * *

Morris slipped in and out of consciousness. The pain in his head made restful sleep impossible. He dreamed about disturbing things, like jumping off a tall building, shooting himself in the face, and, in a particularly vivid dream, stabbing the next person who came through the door wherever he found a vulnerable point in their suit.

In the dream, blood blossomed at the neck of the suit,

and he felt the warmth on his fingers as he pulled his weapon away. What was the weapon? Wasn't clear in the dream.

The suited victim had no face, but they had a voice. They screamed, and then they fell, still screaming, crying out for help. Their shrill cries felt like knives pushing into the base of his skull.

Bodies had rushed in, taken the suited victim away, but never returned.

Morris opened his eyes. The room was dark. Curtains drawn. He glanced to his right.

Dark blob.

Door closed.

He had to piss. The sensation was almost painful. Groaning, Morris pushed himself up. He sat on the edge of the bed, willing the world to stop spinning. He put a foot on the floor. Cold. The feeling wasn't unpleasant, though. That coolness would make his head feel better.

Morris stood. His legs trembled, threatening to buckle under him, but he managed a step. Then two more. It seemed like it took an eternity, but he finally made it to the plastic wall of his tent, where they'd placed a bowl on a small table. His bathroom.

He reached for the bowl.

"Shit," he whispered.

Blood. All over his fingers.

The dream...

Morris's legs finally succumbed to weakness, collapsing beneath him.

Still dreaming. That had to be it. He didn't hurt someone.

Couldn't...

As his cheek touched the cold tiles, Morris let exhaustion claim him. When he woke, he knew the whole nightmare would end.

And that person in the suit would be fine.

* * *

"Why are you doing this?" George asked.

Catherine pressed more gauze over Josiah's wound. "Because he's dying?"

"He's been exposed. Letting him die would be a mercy."

"We still have no definite idea how it's spread. He might be fine, if I can stop the bleeding."

She would never be able to stitch the wound wearing these gloves. If she took them off, though, George would put someone else in charge, because exposure meant the death camp they were quaintly referring to as "quarantine." The only hope any of them had was for her to find a way to kill the parasite that didn't involve killing the patient.

Josiah touched her arm. She pressed the gauze harder on the wound. He shook his head.

"*Sss...*" he said and then choked on the blood in his mouth.

"It's okay, Josiah," she whispered. "You'll be fine."

He shook his head. "Stop."

Catherine pressed her lips together. She fumbled with the needle passed through the decontamination chamber by a nurse.

"No." Josiah pushed at her other hand. "Rather..." he choked again. "Want to die."

"Let him go," George said. He touched her hand, stopping her useless attempt at gripping the needle. "He doesn't want this."

"He doesn't understand. He's in shock."

"Stop," Josiah said again. "It's okay."

Catherine closed her eyes. Josiah choked, and then wheezed. It went against everything in her, but she didn't move as he slowly bled out. Tears threatened, but she wouldn't let them fall. Not in front of George and his goons.

Everyone was silent.

Josiah just finished his internship at the CDC and he'd

barely worked a month as an official employee. Hell, she didn't know if he'd collected a single paycheck yet.

"You have to let them all die," George finally said. "They're dangerous."

"Dr. Jenkins was delirious. He'd never have attacked Josiah if he weren't infected."

A sigh. "I know that. This is what I've been trying to explain to you. That parasite affects their brain chemistry somehow. It changes them."

"But if we can develop a cure—"

"There isn't one. Won't ever be one. It is alien material, Dr. Fairchild. We have no defense against it, other than to remove its food source."

She covered Josiah's face with a sheet and then turned from the bed. Without a word, Catherine walked to the door. She calmly opened it, walked out, and then waited for it to close behind her.

"Catherine," George said, inches from her ear.

"No." Catherine said.

Outside the tent they'd stepped into, a nurse outside pressed a button on the wall. Catherine closed her eyes as the mist, which contained chemical agents that removed almost every bacterium known to man from their suits, sprayed from the jets located on all sides of the tent. She began removing her suit after the mist stopped. She couldn't dislodge the clasp holding her helmet on, though.

"Let me," George said.

She lowered her hands as he opened the clasp and then lifted the helmet from her head.

"Would you?" he asked, turning his back to her.

Catherine sighed and returned the favor. They left their gear on the rack next to the door, and then waited. The nurse outside pressed the button again. The mist filled the chamber again, a secondary precaution, probably unnecessary. When it dissipated, Catherine unzipped the flap that served as a door and then stepped outside the tent. She turned right, intending to hide in her office where she could privately mourn for Josiah and his family.

"Catherine," George said again.

Apparently, she wouldn't be able to crumble just yet.

She let him follow her into the office. Still not capable of words, Catherine walked around the desk and then sat down. George took the chair opposite her desk.

"You know he should've been with the others," he said.

"I needed him close. He has vital information about the pathogen."

"Parasite."

She scowled.

George sighed. "The infection will not get better. I know you want to find a cure, but there isn't one."

"Have you even tried?"

"Of course we have," George said. "For years we tried, but it is incurable."

Nothing was incurable. In her experience, the only thing stopping people from being well was red tape. "I refuse to accept that."

He stood, smoothing his suit jacket. "It's time to put your big girl pants on, dear."

"Stop patronizing me. I'm not a child and this isn't the fifties, where you can speak to me like I'm a hysterical female."

"I'm sorry. I didn't mean it like that."

She shuffled the papers on her desk. "Please get out. I just need a few moments alone."

"I wanted to allow you to come to the right conclusion on your own, but I see you're going to hold on to fairy tales. We've quarantined all but a couple of the potential hosts, and the order has been given to euthanize anyone who has progressed past stage two."

"What? We haven't identified stages."

"You haven't, but we did so a long time ago. Stage one is infection, where the patient is asymptomatic. Stage two, symptoms appear, but there is no personality change. Stage three, suicidal thoughts, aggression, you know the drill. They are not to progress to stage four."

"Which is?"

"Your pet has reached stage four. He's probably approaching the fifth and final stage, which is unacceptable. I will be ordering your team to begin euthanization."

"They won't listen to you."

George smiled as he opened the door. "They already have."

CHAPTER 12

The motel Rachel stayed in had thin walls and shag carpet. The pillows were wrapped in plastic, and a long strip of duct tape held the yellow bedsheet together. She tried to ignore that but found it impossible not to mind the cockroach that scurried under the radiator when she set her bag on the floor next to a ripped brown chair that looked like it'd been stolen from a doctor's waiting room in 1980. She wasn't sure how the place got past health inspections, but at least it allowed her to get a few hours of sleep, fully clothed, with her jacket wrapped around her head to prevent bed bugs from crawling in her ears.

She got up early, showered in her socks, because the stains in the tub look organic and she didn't want some kind of fungus killing her before she could help Morris.

Dr. Fairchild hadn't thought to check Morris's cloud files, so Rachel was able to download several onto her laptop. It took a while, though, thanks to the hotel's dodgy internet connection. No matter how long she stared at the lab results and notes made by Morris over the past couple of months, she couldn't see why the CDC, or whoever those suited goons worked for, would round people up like they were. The parasite was transmittable, but it had to be through physical contact, most likely only through bodily fluids. And even if it were easily transmitted, infection wasn't lethal on its own. The personality changes were the biggest problem. Simple matter of finding the right medication, as Morris hypothesized weeks ago.

A door slammed somewhere outside. She jumped, waited several seconds, listening for movement outside the window, but then told herself to stop being silly. She probably wasn't a priority for the CDC. Not even sick. Sure, she'd had headaches for a couple of days, but she often got those when stressed. They weren't migraines and a couple of aspirins and some sleep usually took care of them. She doubted Dr. Fairchild would agree with her self-diagnosis, though.

Rachel tapped her chin as she ran a search for migraine headaches and quarantines. The only article to appear was a blog post written by a man using a pseudonym. He claimed that his sister had gone to the hospital with a migraine a few days ago, but never returned home, and the hospital refused to give his family any information. The blog seemed to follow an anti-government, conspiracy nut theme, so of course, his story then turned into something any sane person would dismiss as the ramblings of a man with too much time on his hands.

She clicked "latest post" and a frisson of dread crept over her skin.

"Headache is almost unbearable," the man wrote. *"Sometimes hard to form thoughts. Can't speak. Writing this taking forever, but someone has to know. Want to hurt myself. Other people. It is hard to stop myself from giving in to these urges.*

"They've poisoned us, comrades, and I'm afraid I won't be well enough to fight them off if they come. They've called. The hospital. Want me. Quarantine. Going to" the post ended.

Seven hundred and nine comments had been posted beneath. Most urged him to stay strong. Some asked what happened. Where was he? Please respond.

Had the CDC collected him after his sister's admission to the quarantine unit? Probably. Or, like all lunatics, he offed himself as some kind of "fight the power" thing.

Rachel opened a new search. She found the email

addresses for three local news agencies and then began composing a letter. It had to be calm, rational, and believable. Maybe she should just call one of them... no. They'd know who she was if she did that. She didn't want the CDC goons to find her.

Shouldn't even use her laptop to do this. She closed the computer. The library had laptops they loaned out. She'd use one of those. Log in on their server. Make up an anonymous email and get the word out that way.

The phone next to her bed rang. Shit, she didn't think the ancient artifact even worked. Rachel picked up the receiver. "Hello?"

"Hey, sweetheart," the creepy guy running the front desk drawled. "Got the impression you were trying to stay hid, so thought I'd warn you there's some suits sniffing around. Showed me a picture of you."

"Oh..." Rachel's heart pounded.

"Sent them the opposite way. Other side of the motel. You get me?"

"I—yes. Thank you."

"Get gone before they come back and I gotta give them your real room number. They don't look like the type to fuck around."

"I will. Again, thank you."

Rachel put the receiver back on its base and then grabbed her backpack and keys. She opened the door, peeked outside briefly before running toward her car. As she threw herself in the driver's seat, she heard a man shouting.

"Fuck," she whispered as she started the car.

Three men in black suits ran around the right side of the motel. On the left, near her room, another man ran toward her car. Rachel pressed the gas hard and sped out of the parking lot. She didn't stop to look for other cars as she pulled onto the highway and got several angry honks in protest of her carelessness.

While she wasn't a master spy, she knew a few basics

about staying off the radar. She'd withdrawn money from an ATM near the university, miles away from the hotel, and then paid for the room with cash. She hadn't logged onto social media or even her email, so how did they find her?

She finally let out the breath she held when the motel disappeared in her rearview. They probably tracked her license plate. She'd have to find another vehicle or change hers somehow.

As she turned off the freeway onto a one-way street, Rachel realized she left the laptop on the bed. "No big deal," she told herself, taking a left turn onto a road that narrowed into one lane. Still had credit cards, a bit of cash, and the burner phone she bought.

She turned right. The only person she could trust who was close enough to be of any help was her cousin Josie, who lived at the end of this road. Josie gave up a promising law career to be a trophy wife to a trust fund brat who just seemed to get richer. She and Rachel never saw eye-to-eye about life choices the other had made, but Josie had always been s loyal friend. She'd help. Maybe she wouldn't be thrilled about letting Rachel take one of her husband's precious cars, but once she heard the whole story, she'd find a way to ensure he didn't freak out. Matt was an asshole, but he typically let Josie have whatever she wanted.

Rachel just hoped she got out of there before the feds started tracking down family members. As she got out of her car, a jolt of heat tore through her temples, followed by a throbbing at the base of her neck.

She closed her eyes. Stress headache. Got them all the time. After a few seconds, the headache dissipated and Rachel smiled. She never even touched a single patient, not without gloves. Infection was impossible.

Except she spoke to Mark after Jenny's brain exploded without a mask. Touched the sink in the OR, without gloves.

She'd just left her biological material—hair, skin, saliva—all over that motel room. If she were infected, whoever went in there next could get sick, and then whoever they contacted next would also get sick.

She should go into quarantine. It's the right thing to do. *And you'll die. Don't do it.*

Rachel knew the voice was imaginary. Her subconscious making sure she survived whatever was happening. Going into quarantine was morally right, but she'd listen to the voice for now. Someone had to know what was going on. Once she'd warned the world about what the CDC was planning, then she'd lock herself away. First, she had to visit her cousin. Get some money. Then, she'd figure out her next steps.

* * *

Something wet touched her cheek. Rachel opened her eyes. Where the hell was she? What...?

She lifted her head. Blinked. It was dark again. How long had she been sleeping... in an alley? The brick wall on the right side of her looked ready to crumble at any minute. The fire escape leading up toward a half-lit neon sign advertising "XXX Rentals" was missing several steps.

Rachel sat up. She lifted her hands to rub her eyes. Blood coated her fingers. It was dry, flaking off, but unmistakable.

"Run," a voice whispered.

She shook her head. The voice had to be part of whatever she'd been dreaming. A lingering echo in her foggy mind.

The last thing she remembered was Josie answering her door. They'd talked. Rachel asked for aspirin, as the headache that'd come and gone since this shit show started intensified. Josie got her some, and when Rachel asked for the car, she'd asked why she needed it. Then Rachel told her everything.

And Josie didn't look surprised. In fact, she finished a couple of Rachel's sentences for her and then patted her shoulder, keeping an arm's length between them.

"I know," she'd said. "They called me. Asked if you'd

been here. Of course, I said no."

"What did they want?"

"You're sick, hon."

Rachel then realized Josie had done something terrible, but her mind refused to recall what it was or how she'd dealt with it. Was it Josie's blood?

No way would she have hurt Josie. The blood could be anyone's, even her own.

But Rachel couldn't find any injuries on her body.

She picked up her backpack. It was heavier than she remembered. She opened the zipper and looked inside.

"Holy fuck," she said, touching the numerous bills stuffed inside. Had Josie loaned her cash? Why would she just give her wads of it like this? Who kept this kind of money lying around?

"Go," the voice whispered. "You aren't safe."

Rachel stood on shaky legs. She took the cell phone from the front pocket of the bag and turned it on. The date on the screen couldn't be right. No way had she lost two days.

After tucking the phone in her pocket, she lifted the backpack over her shoulder. The best course of action was to find a motel and lock herself inside until she was certain she wouldn't hurt anyone. Whatever happened in the hours that she'd lost, Rachel knew the blood wasn't hers and that meant one thing.

She was infected.

* * *

Morris kept his eyes closed, although the headaches had all but stopped. The pain returned every few hours. Still intense. Still debilitating. But it only lasted a few minutes, and then he felt clear again. Almost normal, if not for the fatigue.

"He's withdrawn," he heard Catherine say. "Seems to be improving, but there's something... no point in telling

George."

The door was still closed. No one had entered the room since he'd attacked the doctor. No one even bothered to ask if he was okay. So, he knew he couldn't be hearing Catherine. Maybe he was hallucinating. The migraines might be so severe he couldn't feel the pain, because he was delirious.

Morris opened his eyes. The room was dark.

"Fucking bullshit," a strange voice said. "Media gets wind of this and we're all fucked."

"Gotta decide," another voice said. "Jason is hot, but Paul doesn't talk like a frat boy. Paul's got money too."

What was he hearing? A radio? Television?

"This one's next." He recognized that voice. George, Catherine called him. The G-man. "Don't care how much research he did. He knows too much. Already too close to stage five. I'll take care of him when Catherine leaves. Take care of her too if she raises a fuss. This nightmare has gone on long enough."

Although he had to be imagining what he heard, rage still bubbled in Morris's belly. Fucking arrogant government pricks. Take over his study, his lab; took his whole fucking hospital. Who the hell were they? Didn't know shit about the parasite or what it could do.

"End him," a voice said.

"Yeah," Morris whispered.

Somehow, he knew George stood outside the door. A gut instinct said if he could just get past the door...

Morris imagined throwing a chair through the glass window hidden by the thick drapes. He pictured it shattering, covering George G-Man in tiny shards.

He heard the pieces hit the ground. A shout. Sounded just like George.

"Rest," the voice said.

* * *

Catherine walked beside George. He rambled about responsibility and sacrifice, but she wasn't really listening. Her mind kept playing the details of the past few days. What had she missed? Morris had been docile, although not impressed about his isolation. He understood.

Why would he attack someone who was just trying to help him?

George shouted, bringing her out of her thoughts.

"Shit," Catherine whispered when she saw the glass. "How did that happen?"

George brushed the shards from his shoulders and pointed into the room beyond the broken glass. Morris lay in the bed, eyes closed. The smile on his face, though, sent a chill over Catherine's skin.

"He didn't do this," she said. "He's barely strong enough to make it to the bathroom."

"Oh, he did it," George said.

"Come on. That glass was—"

"Tempered?"

"Yes. Designed to resist breaking without a significant amount of force."

"And yet, here we are."

She stared at Morris. He slept so peacefully. No way could he have broken the glass and then climbed into bed like that so quickly. "I don't think it was Morris. There has to be another explanation."

George sighed. "We have to euthanize the infected now, starting with Morris and the man down the hall who keeps levitating."

"That was a rumor," Catherine said. "No one but your men saw him do that."

"So, my men are liars?"

"I'm not..." Catherine took a breath. "I know what they think they saw, but it's not possible. Even if he did levitate, which is absurd, I haven't determined which of these patients are suffering regular migraines, and which are infected. We can't euthanize them all."

George pointed to the man guarding Morris's room. "You. Get someone here to fix this glass now. I want two men watching him at all times. If he tries to leave before the window is repaired, shoot him. If he gets out of that bed, shoot him. Do not let him get close to anyone. Clear?"

"Yes, sir."

"George—"

"We're done discussing this for now, Catherine. I have something to show you."

CHAPTER 13

Catherine's instinct was to run when George took her up to the roof of the hospital, where a helicopter waited, but she didn't. She told herself the instinct was silly. Aside from his misguided sense of duty he felt to his country, he had never given her reason to fear him. She had to stop seeing conspiracies around every corner. Yes, he wanted to kill her patients, but his motivation for doing so wasn't sinister. George genuinely believed he was saving the rest of the world, even if he was mistaken about the danger associated with the parasite.

The ride lasted thirty minutes, and when they landed, George escorted Catherine into a large facility built into the base of a mountain.

"Is this a military base?"

He smiled as he put his finger over a red light next to the door. "Something like that."

The door opened and George waved her inside. Catherine hesitated, but only briefly. She walked in, waited for George to put his finger on another red light, and then followed him to a bank of elevators in an empty lobby.

"Where are we going?" she asked when he pressed a white, unmarked button at the bottom of the elevator's keypad.

George pressed several numbers on the keypad and the elevator moved downward. "You'll see. I don't need to tell you that what I'm showing you is highly classified. Speaking of it to anyone could result in prosecution... or worse."

She nodded.

"Good. I'd hate to see anything happen to you. This is something I didn't want to do, but you're stubborn. You have to see the whole picture, apparently."

"What is this place?"

"A research facility, mostly. Nothing evil, I promise."

She smiled, although she knew he was lying. Everything about the placed screamed "evil."

The elevator stopped and the doors opened. A guard clad in the same black uniform as the men George brought to the hospital stood, gun ready. He lowered his weapon when he saw them.

"Sir," he said, saluting George. "We received word of your arrival just a few minutes ago. The subject hasn't been prepped."

"That's okay," George said. "We're just viewing today."

"Understood, sir. Will you require an escort?"

"No. Thank you."

The man nodded and then returned to his post next to the elevator. George touched Catherine's arm and directed her down the hallway. They turned twice, and then George punched a long code into a keypad next to a set of steel doors. He then leaned forward and pressed his eye to a small opening near the top.

"Retinal scans," she said. "Fancy."

"This area isn't even accessible to the President," he said. "Only a handful of people know what we do here."

"So, I should feel honored?"

"What you're about to see will change how you look at everything. I'm afraid it might not be for the better either."

They entered the room beyond the door, and Catherine tried not to gasp. It wasn't a large space, maybe the size of two large bedrooms. On one side, a small lab had been set up with computers, desks, various racks of test tubes and machines. On the other, a glass enclosure extended almost the entire length of the room.

"Come on," George said.

Catherine followed him to the enclosure. Behind the glass, or maybe within it, she couldn't tell for sure, were thick steel bars. They passed what looked like a sitting room, and then a bathroom. She stared at the contents of the enclosure, memorizing every detail. A thin, barely discernable light danced over the glass now and then.

"Well, well," a man said. "It's been a while, young George."

George said nothing as they reached the end of the enclosure. A man sat on a bed, book in his hands. He wore a white shirt and white pants, no shoes, and his dark hair was overgrown, messy, but that didn't diminish his attractiveness.

She looked at George for an explanation.

"This is Charles," George said. "My great grandfather."

"Bullshit." Catherine didn't know what he was trying to prove, but the man in the strange glass prison was younger than both of them. She'd guess him to be mid to late thirties at the most.

"I wish it was," George said.

"How is that possible?"

"Charles was the closest neighbor to the Baker plantation. After the family fell ill, and he assisted the clergy in burning the infected, he left the area. He didn't tell his wife, my great grandmother, who raised their children alone after he abandoned them."

"I feared for their lives," Charles said from behind the glass. "If I'd known the truth, I may have stayed, although I doubt the children would have survived, so perhaps it worked out as it should have. If they'd died, you wouldn't exist."

George ignored Charles, continuing with his story. "Charles left because he started getting headaches like the Bakers suffered before they went insane. He was afraid they'd burn him as well."

"Not just burn me," Charles said. "They'd have burned

me alive, because they feared getting too close to the infected to put us down mercifully. Not a fate anyone desires."

"He went as far away as he could manage," George said, not looking at Charles. "Considering the debilitating nature of his symptoms, he didn't get far. Suffered for weeks, he claims, and just when he thought it was done, and he would finally die, he didn't."

"Now, Georgie, that's not the whole story." Charles stood. He walked to the glass wall, stopping just shy of touching it.

The thin blue lights Catherine noticed earlier spidered over the glass near his body.

"Is this electrified?" she asked.

Charles smiled. "Yes. Wouldn't want the animal escaping the zoo."

"Because the *animal* kills people," George said. "He's dangerous, Catherine. Don't be fooled by his charm."

She shook her head. "I wasn't—I don't understand any of this."

"We discovered that electricity prevents him from using his powers, for lack of a better word to describe what he can do. He can't break the glass to escape, nor can he harm anyone outside his cell. The bars are there if we have a power failure and he does manage to break the glass."

"Seems a little extreme for one person."

"A necessary precaution. Trust me."

"Georgie is the most trustworthy man I know," Charles said. "Honest, loyal to a fault, and forever in the pursuit of justice. Makes me proud."

"He's not—it's not possible for him to be who you think he is."

"Yes, it is," Charles said. "George is the son of my granddaughter. I've followed my descendants as closely as I could, but when I found George, I thought I'd found the perfect candidate."

"For what?" Catherine asked.

"The next generation."

"I don't understand."

"I let him find me. Showed him what I could do." He pointed to the glass separating them. "This is the thanks I get for it."

George shook his head. "Let's not go down this road. It never ends and we don't have time for it."

"Rather than being happy to find his long-lost relative," Charles continued. "He believes himself duty-bound to stop me from destroying the world, or some nonsense like that. I merely want to live a normal life."

"While infecting innocent people." George touched Catherine's arm. "He killed hundreds before we found him. He says he was trying to help some of them, but no one survived his "help." Thankfully, there's no one else out there with his abilities."

"That was before I realized the parasite required a specific type of host," Charles said. "And once one progresses to my stage, the parasite, as you call it, is too powerful for the average body to accommodate. Infection must come from, what did you call the ones in the dirt?"

"First generation."

"Right. Anyway, I wanted to give others the gift I've received. I never wanted to hurt them. If I could change what happened, I would. Sadly, time travel is not one of my abilities." He smiled. "Yet."

"You knew what the parasite would do and the kind of suffering people would endure, but you still *intentionally* infected people?" Catherine tried to keep the disdain from her voice but failed.

"I believe the suffering is worth the reward. The parasite evolves with each new host. It adapts as it learns what kills the host and what doesn't. As with any living organism, it doesn't want to lose its only means of survival. With each new host, I noticed a shorter incubation period and the symptoms became less severe. I thought that in time one or two would come through it, as I did."

"You were wrong, I assume."

"Yes. While the parasite is smart and adaptable, it can't account for the fragility of the human body. I didn't realize the odds of survival depended on the host in the end."

"And yet," George said. "He continued to infect people after realizing this."

Catherine couldn't digest all the information they gave her. "Why did you continue if you knew it would kill them?"

"What's that saying? To make an omelet, you've gotta crack a few eggs. I knew that, eventually, I'd find a perfect host. With that host would come answers that would ensure finding subsequent hosts wouldn't result in as many casualties."

"What good could this parasite possibly do for someone?"

Charles grinned. "Oh, I don't know. Immortality is pretty great."

"This is nonsense." She turned to George. "This man is clearly insane. I'm starting to wonder about your mental stability as well."

George sighed. "Show Catherine what you can do, Charles, so she might fully understand what we're up against."

"This might be your zoo, son, but I'm not your monkey."

"I know you want to. Please, just show her something."

Charles examined his nails and then smoothed a wrinkle in the front of his shirt. "What's in it for me?"

"Perhaps I can see about getting that iPad you're so enamored with."

"And Internet?"

"Limited, as long as I can get approval."

Charles stared, but Catherine could see the desire in his eyes. If he truly were as old as George claimed, modern technology would seem almost magical. Still, she suspected he was too smart to be bought so easily. He *wanted* to show her what he could do.

Charles smiled and then waved his hand. The bed behind him overturned. He tilted his head to the right, and a book flew from the small shelf opposite the bed.

"He's telekinetic?" Catherine said.

"And clairvoyant, precognitive, psychometric, and telepathic," George said. "We believe he might also be psychokinetic, but he refuses to cooperate with our tests."

"What is that?"

"The ability to influence the minds of others," Charles said. "They believe I can contact people far away from here and alter their thoughts. Make them believe things merely by saying it's true. Absurd, right?"

"It's impossible."

"We've proven he can read minds, move objects without touching them, and he can divine information from a person or object by touching it. Why would the ability to communicate over long distances or alter a person's thoughts be impossible if all of that is true?"

"But how?" Catherine asked.

"No one truly understands abilities like his. We're trying, though."

"I mean how is he still alive? How did he develop these abilities?"

"As Charles said, the parasite doesn't kill all of its hosts," George explained. "Those who don't kill themselves or suffer a stroke, heart attack or other fatal event due to the severity of the symptoms, become something different. Something inhuman."

"Come on," Charles said. "I'm still human."

"Not exactly," George said. "He kept a journal through his illness, which was found with his effects when the government tracked him down in the fifties. He managed to escape that time, but we gathered a lot of information in that journal. It's how I found him later."

"I let you find me. Let's keep to the facts, Georgie."

George ignored Charles. "He's more than one hundred years old, yet his body hasn't aged a day. As the parasite reproduced in his body, it should have killed him, but once he reached stage four, something different happened. We believe he might be immortal, or damn close to it."

Catherine laughed. "*That* is impossible."

"We ran the DNA tests, Catherine. My great grandmother kept an old hat he was fond of wearing. We found his hair inside the brim and ran tests. It's his hair and he is my grandfather."

"He might be related, but that doesn't mean he's your great grandfather. If he were from the same family, perhaps a cousin on your grandmother's side that you might not know about, mitochondrial DNA would be identical."

"The follicles were intact, and our mitochondrial DNA isn't identical, which means he is not a cousin, or a distant relative on my great grandmother's side. He's not related to her at all. He was her husband. There is no doubt as to his identity."

"It's ridiculous. No one can live that long without aging."

George patted her shoulder. "I have more for you to see, and then you might not find what I'm telling you so difficult to believe, but not in front of him. He uses every drop of information, no matter how irrelevant it seems, to his advantage."

"Wait. You can't leave so soon," Charles said. "What's happened, Georgie? Why is she here with you?"

"She's a new employee," George lied. "Don't get excited."

"No, that's not true. She's here because there are more," Charles said. "Someone found it. How many are sick?"

"No one found anything. Come, Catherine."

George pushed Catherine toward the door. As they left, she heard Charles laughing.

"I told you there'd be more," he yelled. "You'll never stop it."

George didn't reply. They left the room. He led

Catherine back the way they came and to a black door. A fingerprint was all they required to get into this one. It was a sparsely decorated office. George flipped on the light and pointed to a chair behind a grey metal desk. He opened the laptop that was the only thing on the desk and then typed a login and password into it. She watched as he opened a video file.

"Just watch," he said, standing back.

The video was grainy, but she could tell it was recorded decades earlier. The glasses worn by the nurse and the uniforms indicated it might have been 1950, possibly 1960. A man wearing scrubs mopped the floor near Charles's cell, which was a typical jail cell; iron bars and no top.

Charles leaned against the bars. She stared at his face. The same as the one she saw just moments ago. Impossible... yet there he was.

In the video, Charles whispered something. The man mopping the floor glanced at him, said something in reply. Charles smiled. As the man left the area in front of Charles's cell, his head exploded. Blood covered the floor he just mopped, and his body remained standing for a moment, before crumpling. Charles laughed. People ran toward the poor man, but they stopped just a few feet away.

"Jesus Christ," Catherine said.

"You see now?" George asked. "He's dangerous."

She nodded. "So, he could have—"

"No. The glass is electrified, as I explained. Took a while, but we figured out that the electric current prevents him from using his power, for lack of a better term."

"This is insane."

"I don't disagree. Do you understand now? They must not survive infection, Catherine, or we'll have a mob of invincible killers on our hands."

"But how?"

George reached across the desk. He clicked on another file and then stood back. "Go ahead. Look."

Catherine opened the subfolder and then opened the first image file. "Is this—?"

"Charles. Yes."

"There are... Jesus Christ, it's not possible."

"The parasite is in every vein, every organ, every fiber of his being," George confirmed. "It takes over, so that the person they were before is no longer there. The Charles you see today is not the Charles who abandoned his family in order to spare their lives. He's someone different. *Something* different."

"But he can't live like this. Human biology is—"

"Yet, he's alive. Thriving, actually."

"It defies logic."

"I know. This is overwhelming and extremely difficult to process, but I needed you to understand what we're up against here. We're not killing people, my dear. We're eliminating potential hosts for a monster we have no idea how to fight. Hell, we don't even know where the parasite came from or what it or the beings who left it want."

"Why keep him alive? He's dangerous, obviously. If you're studying him for answers, I'd say the risk isn't worth the reward."

"Honestly, for a long time, we just didn't know how to kill him. After a while, we decided that he could be useful. If only we could trust him."

"Do you think that's possible?"

George closed the laptop. "No, but a bit of hope never hurt anyone. He just needs the right motivation."

CHAPTER 14

Rachel stole a car. She'd walked to a gas station after leaving the alley, broke into the restroom to wash the blood from her hands and clothes. Her jacket was unsalvageable, so she'd left that in the trash. Blood still stained her jeans and the bottom of her t-shirt, so she'd used some of the money in the backpack to buy new clothes. If the clerk at the store noticed the blood, she didn't give any indication of it.

As Rachel exited the store wearing her new clean clothes, she saw the car idling at the curb outside. Almost like the owner *wanted* it to be stolen. She just got in, checked the rearview, and then drove away. No one ran after her.

Nothing happened.

Somehow, she knew it'd be okay, like a strange force guided and protected her. She'd have called it instinct, but it didn't feel the same. It came from somewhere inside her head, not her gut. A silent voice that pushed her in the right directions.

As her initial fear over stealing a car faded, that silent voice warned that the owner wouldn't wait to report it stolen, so she didn't have much time before the cops had the plate number. She had to make sure when they saw the plates, they weren't on the car she was driving.

At a stoplight, she noticed a sign announcing free parking. Rachel turned right and then drove the short distance to the almost empty lot. The section near the back was poorly lit, thanks to the shadow of a tall building. She parked next to a similar car in the same shade of grey as the one she stole.

The seconds ticked by too fast as she surveilled the parking lot to make sure no one watched her. Confident she wouldn't be seen, Rachel quickly removed the plates from her new car, and then switched them with the other. Somehow, again, her luck held out.

Rachel drove for a long time, thinking, planning, and finally became aware of her surroundings while driving through the side streets of the undeveloped area at the north end of the city. Houses were dilapidated, if she were being generous about their condition. Many homes were little more than trailers plopped onto a small strip of land. A few single-story structures had been built decades before and were in various states of disrepair. A couple had weathered house wrap covering the outer walls, as though someone once thought they might replace the siding, and then changed their minds half-way through the process. Many had plastic sheets protecting broken windows, or plywood covering the opening entirely. One home had shingles over most of the roof, and then steel across a small sunken section at the front.

The homeowners made the properties look as nice as they could, though, despite the obvious lack of funds and/or resources to do so. Some erected short fences, painted them pretty colors, planted flower gardens, or purchased colorful lawn furniture to draw the eye away from the sad structures and patchy brown grass and dirt that overwhelmed the plots of land.

She drove through this area, turning, backtracking, turning again, until she felt almost certain no one followed her. Then she stopped at a convenience store and rested her head on the steering wheel.

Morris could be dead for all she knew, and this game of cat and mouse meant nothing. She knew she was symptomatic, although the headaches she'd had didn't follow a pattern like the others. Even if she weren't sick, if Morris didn't back up the information she planned to share with the media, they would never believe her. She was one person. A student. No degrees to give her words weight. No studies of her own under her belt. She assisted Morris in the lab, but he never shared much until recently, and what she knew made no sense to her. How would it sound to someone who knew nothing about the science behind migraine clusters?

At least she didn't have a headache anymore. It'd disappeared soon after she found the car. Had to be stress related. The cluster headaches held on for days, not hours.

But what about the days you can't remember?

Rachel lifted her head. A light had gone out on the store's sign. In the dimness of dusk, it appeared nonsensical. "ICK STOP" it read. Tiny bugs whorled around the lit section. She watched them spiral up, out, and then down, repeating the pattern over and over. It occurred to her she'd never noticed such a thing before. Then again, she'd never watched bugs fly around a light with much interest either.

Now and then, as a customer went in or out, a cow-bell clanged. Somewhere beyond the store, music played. Heavy. Screamy. She smelled barbeque and gasoline.

Rachel rubbed her eyes. What did she do now?

"Help me," someone said.

The voice was so solid, so real, she turned to check the backseat.

"Not much time," it continued.

"Where are you?" she whispered but knew the answer. The voice came from her own head. It'd been whispering since she woke in the alley, but she ignored it, blaming the headache.

The headache was gone now, though.

"Go south."

She stared at her reflection in the rearview. Her hair was disheveled, eyes red. She needed sleep. Food. The cow bell clanged, drawing her attention to the store.

Maybe the voice was her own. Something subconscious

that kept her out of the CDC's hands up to this point. Nothing to lose by listening to it. She could use a burner phone to call someone. A local news agency. Toss it away after, and then use another to try to reach Morris. She had all that cash in the backpack. Might as well use it, rather than agonize over how it came into her possession.

Doing something was better than doing nothing.

Rachel opened the backpack, took out a wad of bills, and then opened the car door. She scanned the small parking lot and the adjoining street as she exited. A man in a white hoodie walked on the opposite side of the road. Hands in his pockets, he didn't look her way. She waited until he disappeared down the street, just to be safe, and then went into the store.

The kid behind the counter couldn't have been more than sixteen. Her greasy hair was pulled high on her head in one of those ridiculous buns Rachel noticed other girls at the university wearing. From the door, her face appeared smooth and pale, but as she approached the counter, Rachel realized she'd used layers of makeup to conceal numerous bumps. She wanted to tell girls like this that if they stopped using so much makeup, those bumps would disappear, but it was none of her business. Let them feed the beauty industry as all the women before them have done. Not her problem.

The girl stared at the phone in her hand, not even blinking as Rachel stood across from her.

Rachel cleared her throat.

The girl sighed, but she didn't look up.

"Do you have prepaid phones?" Rachel asked.

The girl pointed to her left. "Next to the gift cards," she said and then resumed texting.

Rachel walked toward the rack of gift cards that had been unwisely placed next to the door. On the left side of that, she saw a tall, narrow display of cell phones. She perused the selection. Didn't need anything fancy, she supposed. She grabbed four of the cheapest ones, and then checked the provider for each before scooping up several prepaid phone cards as well.

The girl continued to stare at her phone as Rachel picked up a case of bottled water, some chips and chocolate bars, and a couple of sandwiches out of the small refrigerator next to the coffee machines. Oh, coffee would be amazing, even if it'd been sitting all day, which, given the girl's total disinterest in doing her job, it probably had.

Rachel dumped her items on the counter. The girl sighed, set the phone down, and started scanning the items before tossing them, almost angrily, into a bag.

"I'm just going to grab a coffee as well."

"Sure," the girl said.

"Extra-large."

"Yep."

Rachel made her coffee and returned to the counter before the girl finished scanning her items.

"Little early for Christmas shopping," the girl said.

"Pardon?"

"Phones?"

"Oh," Rachel's eye was drawn to the television next to the counter. She recognized Dr. Fairchild standing in front of the hospital. "Birthday gifts. I have a lot of nieces and nephews. Can you turn that up?"

The girl glanced at the television. "Why?"

"I know her. Simply curious what it's about."

The girl reached behind the counter and then pointed a remote control at the television.

"This is not an epidemic," Dr. Fairchild said. "I cannot stress enough the need for everyone to be calm. We are trying to prevent an outbreak by asking anyone with the symptoms listed a minute ago to seek medical attention immediately. If you are infected by C-1, it is important to get treatment as early as possible."

C-1? The parasite had a name now. Hopefully, that meant they'd made progress in at least identifying its origins.

Did they have a cure? Rachel frowned. No way.

Three men in black suits stood next to Dr. Fairchild. One man, whose eyes made Rachel's blood turn cold, stared at Dr. Fairchild's back. His expression gave no indication of his thoughts or feelings on what the doctor was saying.

"Is it true that people are dying from this infection?" someone asked.

Dr. Fairchild glanced at the man behind her, who nodded, and then turned to the cameras again. "There have been some deaths, but these were due to unrelated, pre-existing conditions, and suicide. The virus itself has not yet caused death, but without treatment, we believe it could."

"There were reports online of forced confinement for patients who willingly came to the hospital seeking treatment, as well as teams of medical personnel abducting people from their homes who are not symptomatic. Can you comment on this?"

Rachel bit her lip. She should've known the general public would get the word out. It both relieved and scared her. A panicked population was almost worse than an ignorant one.

"That's two hundred eight, ma'am," the girl at the counter said.

Rachel nodded but made no move to get the money from her pocket. She watched the television instead, waiting for Dr. Fairchild's answer.

Dr. Fairchild looked at the man again. He nodded almost imperceptibly. Why look to him for answers? Dr. Fairchild was the team leader. She was the expert. This guy was just... Rachel didn't know what he was. Some government goon, she'd bet.

"That is false," Dr. Fairchild said. "We received calls from patients and their family members, all requesting medical assistance, and that is the only time we have gone to anyone's home."

A lie. They came after Rachel at the motel. She had no

doubt they'd have abducted her if she'd stayed.

"In some cases," Dr. Fairchild continued. "Patients were afraid to seek treatment, due to the costs involved I imagine, and refused to go to a hospital. When we made it clear that treatment was free, they consented to quarantine to protect their loved ones. No one has been quarantined against their wishes, and no one has been abducted. Again, we are asking for your cooperation in *preventing* an outbreak of epidemic proportions. We want to stop the spread of the virus now, in its early days. There is no need to panic or to fear your doctors. We just want to make sure no one else gets sick."

"Ma'am?"

"And that's something else I want to make clear," Dr. Fairchild said. "The virus is highly contagious, and while it may not be dangerous for one individual, it can be lethal for another. There is no way to know at this point how it will affect each person. So, please seek medical attention if you experience symptoms to avoid spreading the virus to—"

The screen went blank.

Rachel looked up at the girl.

"I have shit to do, ma'am. You gonna pay or what?"

"Sorry," Rachel said. "How much?"

The girl pointed to the register.

Rachel counted out 250 dollars. "Keep the change."

She gathered her items and then left the store. The girl didn't thank her for the extra forty bucks, but Rachel suspected she rarely thanked anyone for anything.

Her heart pounded as she slid into the driver's seat. She tossed her bags in the back. So, someone had leaked information to the media already. Maybe she didn't need Morris to back up her story. She didn't have the files, though. The laptop was now in their hands. Could buy another one, use the library maybe...

"Get out of town."

The voice accompanied a sharp pain down the middle of her forehead. She winced, closing her eyes against the heat accompanying the pain.

"South," she said, mostly to herself.

"South," the voice echoed.

Rachel started the car and then pulled out of the parking lot. She turned left and drove toward the highway. She'd go south until something made sense.

CHAPTER 15

They stuck needles in his arms until he could no longer fight. The sedatives inside those needles weighted his arms and eyelids and stuffed his mouth with cotton. The headaches had almost disappeared but left behind a presence that flowed through his body, leaving him feeling anxious and eager to escape. Thanks to the drugs forced into his veins, he couldn't go anywhere. Couldn't even speak.

For hours, he'd waited for someone to come in and check his vitals. No one came. Not since the glass broke. Five armed men in white suits had circled his bed then and held him down to sedate him into a coma. Since that moment, he'd been helpless.

Hopeless.

A tingling sensation irritated his veins. While it wasn't painful, he didn't find it pleasurable either. It was... unsettling. Like something moved through his blood, invading every cell in his body. Was this how the parasite finally killed him? No one had progressed far enough in his study to know what its ultimate outcome might be.

If the parasite didn't kill him, he knew *they* would. Hadn't they discussed that numerous times right outside his door? Dr. Fairchild argued against it, and for that he was grateful, but he sensed a slow decline in her belief of what was right and wrong. Her last refusal to allow euthanizing had no heart in it. No heat behind the words.

"We're not murderers," she'd said, but not very convincingly.

What did Fairchild know now that she didn't know a few days ago? What could make her waiver in her commitment to her oath to do no harm?

He heard whispers outside... or inside. The voices sounded like they came from deep in his brain, so he couldn't be sure. His perception of everything was skewed. He had no foundation. Down was up, and up was down. At least nothing was sideways.

Morris chuckled to himself. The whole thing went sideways when the CDC showed up.

Did they discover the source of the parasite? Maybe it was incurable. Highly contagious and deadly. Sure, euthanizing the infected would seem wise if that were the case. If doctors actually did that sort of thing. But they didn't. It was wrong. Their job was to help everyone, even the hopeless.

Still, right or wrong, he knew they'd kill him if he didn't figure out how to move despite the restraints holding him down. They feared what the parasite could do, and without a way to kill it, they felt they had no choice but to kill the host.

He understood their fear. Hadn't he felt it himself when examining his study patients?

"They cannot hurt you," a voice whispered. The same voice who'd told him to break the window.

Morris knew he couldn't have broken the glass. He hadn't even touched it. Someone set him up. Wanted him and maybe Dr. Fairchild to think he could touch things with his mind. He didn't know why. Maybe it was George, the G-man who wanted to kill him. Those types knew all kinds of shit about mind control.

"Don't be afraid," the voice said.

Perhaps that voice was hope. The human being's last resource when all became lost. He'd hang onto it, he supposed. Didn't have much else to get him through this.

If death were coming, he'd face it. Accept it. Embrace it even.

"There is nothing to fear," the voice said, louder now. "You can't die."

Morris didn't believe the voice but had no time to dwell on it. He heard a ruckus somewhere beyond his prison. Saw a man wearing a hospital gown trying to break a window. Not with his mind. This man used his own head.

"Good morning," a voice said. "How are we feeling today?"

"*Nguh*," Morris managed through the cotton.

"Ah, the sedative is still hanging on, I see," the voice, a woman's, replied. "Let me help you out there. This should wake you up."

Morris heard a plastic wrapper. Felt a slight tug at the IV site on his hand, and then the fog began to clear. Several seconds passed before he could open his eyes. His mouth still felt dry and full of fuzzy bits.

"Water," he said.

The woman, who wore the standard white suit worn by everyone who entered his room, leaned over, holding a straw to his lips. He sucked hard, taking in as much water as he could.

"Not too much," she said, taking the straw away. "You might vomit."

Morris wanted more but didn't argue with her. He cleared his throat. A little better.

"How is the head?" the woman asked.

"Good," Morris said. His voice sounded scratchy. "No pain."

"Well, that's an improvement."

"Why am I restrained?"

"Because you might harm yourself."

A lie. They worried he'd harm them. Morris let it slide. He could hear the man, wherever he was, screaming. Knew he'd kill himself if someone didn't stop him.

"Do you hear that?" he asked the woman, who busied herself checking Morris's pulse and temperature.

"Hear what?"

"The man."

"What man?"

"He's killing himself."

She stared at him. "Where?"

"Don't know. I can hear him, though." Morris saw him clearly. Didn't know how, but he knew what he saw was happening. At the man's feet, he saw another man. He lay on the floor, arms out, his head under the bed next to them. Blood pooled around his body. "And he's killed someone."

* * *

The quarantine ward was chaotic. Men in black uniforms stood at every door, guns drawn. People in white suits, Catherine's people, ran back and forth. She saw two covered in blood running toward her.

"Dr. Fairchild," one said through her helmet. Catherine recognized Dr. Benton, an overachiever in medical school, and a rising star on her team. She was ambitious, tough, and sometimes, according to coworkers, a little too cold. Right now, she looked like a scared child.

"What?" Catherine prompted, when Benton said no more.

"There's been an incident."

"Imagine that," George muttered somewhere behind them.

Catherine ignored him. "Tell me."

"Patient in room three was decapitated."

"What?"

"His roommate said he asked him to do it. Insisted. So, I guess he just laid down while the other one… I don't know. It doesn't make sense. He said he did it with the bedrail, but we can't figure out how that's even possible."

"Where is the roommate now?"

"Sedated. He tried to jump out the window. It wouldn't

open, so he started bashing his head against the glass. It's tempered, so you can imagine how badly that went."

"I'm telling you, Catherine," George said. "We have to do something now."

"Not yet. Please, just let me do my job."

"I can't if it interferes with mine."

"Dr. Fairchild," Benton said. "There's something else."

Because she needed more shit happening. Catherine closed her eyes. "Well, go on."

"The man from the lab, the researcher you isolated away from everyone else?"

"Morris?"

"Yes."

Shit. What had he done now? "What about him?"

"He warned us this was happening when we checked his vitals. I was going to chalk it up as the ramblings of a fevered brain, but then one of the guards started shouting. It's unbelievable, but he described exactly what happened."

"See?" George touched Catherine's shoulder. "He's already too far gone, I bet. Jesus Christ, this is worst case scenario here. If you allow them to progress—"

"Finish cleaning up," Catherine interrupted. "And then make sure all of the patients are restrained. I don't care if they've been a danger to anyone. I want everyone in their beds."

"Yes, ma'am."

Catherine watched the two white bodies scurry away. George said nothing. Probably because he knew her resolve was weakening. They couldn't cure this, and it was getting out of hand. Who knew how many were still roaming free? They could infect hundreds. Maybe even thousands. Somehow, she had to get a handle on this. Maybe George's plan was the only option. For the dangerous ones anyway...

"Before we start the killing," she said. "I'd like to run down the list of potential known parasites to see if this one is related to one of those. If it is, then we would be able to devise a treatment, and help people get well instead of letting them die."

"You said yourself you've never seen anything like this. How many more tests do you need before you accept that?"

"It is new. That I agree with, but it could be a…" she searched her memory for similar symptoms associated with parasites. "A type of… hairworm we haven't discovered yet, which could be treatable."

"Such as?"

"There's a hairworm common in crickets and grasshoppers that targets their central nervous system. They ingest the larvae by drinking infested water, and when the larvae mature, they release a powerful chemical that causes the host to kill themselves by jumping into a body of water, where the hairworm can escape the host and begin the cycle again."

"Is it transmittable to humans?"

"No."

"Then it's not a hairworm."

"It could be a related species that infects humans. Science hasn't uncovered everything out there, George. Just like us, other organisms evolve to survive. It's impossible to estimate how many unidentified parasites are even out there, waiting to be discovered."

"Let's say it is a hairworm. How does your theory explain Charles?"

"I guess it doesn't, but it might not be the same parasite. I'd like to test Charles's blood against the samples from our patients. It could be something totally different, which means what we're dealing with here might be something we can treat."

"I'd let you do that, but it's not going to give you any answers. This is the same parasite Charles has and it's not from this planet."

"It has to be. Just let me test his blood and compare it to Morris's. If they're similar, then I'll step out of your way."

He sighed. "You're grasping at straws."

She was, but that's how she found solutions. If she pulled enough, eventually one of the straws would have the answer at the end of it. "I know getting Charles's blood is difficult, so if we can't do that, at least give me some time to look into a couple of theories."

"I feel like we should clarify what you mean by "a couple," because you'll go for years trying to prove I'm wrong about the alien thing."

"You are wrong."

"I'm not, but I'll humor you. Give me two of your theories."

She wasn't prepared to list theories she hadn't come up with yet, so it took a few moments to give him something that sounded reasonable. "Uh, well, the symptoms I've seen share traits with granulomatous amebic encephalitis as well, so that's another avenue we should explore before we start euthanizing innocent people."

He slipped his hands into the pockets of his jacket. "And what is that?"

"A parasite that affects the brain. It's usually fatal, though, because it's hard to diagnose and treat. Patients have presented with seizures, brainstem symptoms, and other neurological issues, just like the ones we have in quarantine."

"Would an autopsy support this?"

"It would, but we found no inflammatory necrosis of brain tissue. There were no amoebic cysts or traces of parasites present, either, except for two samples. One that Morris claims contained eggs. Those disintegrated before tests could be conducted. There was another sample I retrieved during an autopsy. I saw the eggs, and was able to isolate them, but they disintegrated before we could run tests."

"Have you ever seen such a thing occur before?"

"No."

"Exactly. This isn't an organism we've ever seen,

because it's not from this planet."

"No, it's one we haven't seen, because it's a mutation of the ones we know. I'm certain we can crack this and treat these people. Just give me a little more time, George."

Down the hall, her team removed a gurney with a black bag on top. She knew she had to figure something out. This couldn't go on.

"I'm not a terrible person," George said. "I usually save lives, but this is beyond us. You won't identify the parasite, nor will you be able to cure anyone infected with it. There is only one solution, and I'm sorry it's not something your conscience is satisfied with. This is a threat we can't be too cautious in dealing with."

She sighed. "Killing people is never the answer. I don't care how big a threat we're dealing with. They're sick. We don't euthanize a sick person. We help them as best we can, and if we can't cure them, we treat their symptoms."

"Must be nice up there in your little castle with the rose-colored windows."

"You don't have to be an asshole."

He smiled. "I'm not. I'm being practical. Look, I'll give you forty-eight hours. We have some loose ends to tie up, and if you haven't identified the parasite in that time, we're going with my plan."

"By loose ends, you mean finding the remaining hosts?"

"We've picked up everyone but Morris's assistant."

"She's probably fine, or she'd have come in on her own. She understands that she can't fight the infection without help."

"Does she?"

"She's a good person."

"Well, we tracked down her cousin. I think she might disagree with you."

"Why? Was she in contact with Rachel? Is she infected? I'd like to speak to her."

He shook his head. "She won't be speaking to anyone.

Rachel contacted her, she called us, and when we got there, the blood covering her kitchen was still warm. Missed her by minutes, I'm thinking. No trace of her now, though."

"Blood?" Catherine couldn't imagine that girl harming a fly.

"I have photos of the scene. I should warn you, though, if you ever want to sleep again, you might want to just believe me without looking at them."

"Maybe it wasn't Rachel. Could've been the cousin was ill and Rachel tried to help her. She may have acted in self-defense or the cousin hurt herself. Self-harm is a common symptom with cluster migraines."

"That's possible."

"Rachel would come to us if she had symptoms," Catherine insisted.

"Unless she's aware of what we're about to do."

"I haven't agreed yet and how would she know?"

"I don't need your approval. The only reason I've waited is because I respect and care about you. I want you to be on board with this, but I won't wait forever. Morris is dangerously close to becoming like Charles. I can't allow that."

"Rachel isn't a concern. I met her. She's smart and responsible. She'd never put others in danger."

"She could be scared, and fear does strange things to a person. The fight or flight instinct often changes one's priorities."

"Maybe," Catherine said. Part of her hoped Rachel was symptomatic, and that she escaped long enough to recover, so they could prove to George infection didn't mean the world was going to end. "Aside from her, we've got everyone else on the list in quarantine?"

"Everyone who may have been in contact with anyone at that site. As I mentioned, the cousin of Morris's assistant—Rachel—was contacted during the early stages. We asked her to let us know if Rachel made contact or if she herself started experiencing headaches."

"Maybe she called because she was sick, and not because Rachel was there."

"No, she said Rachel was on her way."

"Are you sure she didn't kill herself?"

"Oh, she was murdered. Every bone in her body was broken. The blow that killed her though, was the one that shattered the back of her skull. Rachel's fingerprints were all over the scene."

Catherine swallowed against the lump in her throat. "Let me talk to my team. I won't euthanize anyone who isn't showing symptoms."

George laughed. "I'm not thrilled about killing innocent people either, but we have to consider the need for some collateral damage. For the greater good, I mean."

"Collateral damage? I don't understand."

"Well," George said, smoothing his tie. "We have no way of knowing if a person is infected unless they exhibit symptoms or we manage to find the parasite in one of your scans. You know as well as I do that sometimes the little fuckers hide. We've got how many patients that are symptomatic, yet you can't find a single parasite in their bodies?"

She rolled her eyes. "Several, but that could mean they're just suffering from migraines, not infected by the parasite."

"Unlikely," he said. "Even if that were true, some of them are aware of what's happening here. Would you like them to leave this place and tell the world what they witnessed? How well would the world take the knowledge that we did in fact quarantine people against their will?"

Catherine didn't want to harm anyone who wasn't dangerous, but she didn't want anyone telling the world that CDC employees killed sick people. "We can't do this to people who are healthy. I just can't allow it, George. We must make sure they're sick and there's no hope of them getting better before I'll even consider what you're suggesting."

"Don't worry, dear. I'll make sure they're infected."

CHAPTER 16

Rachel found a hotel that didn't care about real names, paid cash, and fell onto the smelly linens covering the bed as soon as she locked the door behind her. She didn't remember closing her eyes, and her dreams were so vivid, she couldn't tell if she was awake or asleep.

She heard a voice, the same one prompting her to hide and guiding her in just how to do that, whispering things. Horrible things. It urged her to find Morris. Help him escape.

Morris was probably already dead.

"Help me," she heard Morris say. "Please, Rachel."

Had to be her subconscious. She felt guilty about leaving him there and now she was torturing herself.

"He's alive," the voice insisted. "You must be ready."

Be ready for what?

Rachel's dreams shifted for a time. Now and then, lights danced behind her eyes and then a stab of pain vibrated through her temples. When the pain faded, she saw people in hospital beds. Their legs and arms were secured by heavy straps. Someone put needles in their arms as they fought to be free. One by one, they stopped fighting as the drugs in the bags connected to their IVs sedated them.

She saw the men in black suits, guns ready, watching the medical personnel closely. One man, the one she remembered from the press conference, walked to the doorway of a room. He said something, but she couldn't hear it. Handed a person in a white suit a tray full of glass bottles.

The person in the white suit held the tray but didn't

move. The man's face changed. It became hard. Mean. He said something again, and the person in the white suit did a sort of half bow, and then returned to the patients in the room. They filled a syringe with the contents of a bottle. Holding it in the air, the white suit person turned, as though making sure of their instructions.

The man in the black suit nodded and the white suit person approached the patient in the bed. They injected the contents of the syringe into the arm of the patient. The man, strapped to the bed so he couldn't fight back, jerked once, and then his face took on a serene quality.

The white suit put a gloved hand to the patient's neck.

Waited.

Rachel held her breath as the white suit person's shoulders sunk just a little, and then they moved to the other bed and prepared another syringe. She tried to wake from the nightmare, but it clung to her mind. It refused to let her turn her eyes from what was happening.

With each person she imagined receiving an injection, she felt the life leaving their bodies as if it were her own death. Over and over again, injection after injection, she suffered the last moments along with them.

Why couldn't she wake up?

"They're killing them all," the voice said. "And you will be next."

Rachel couldn't breathe. A fire sparked in her head. Its heat spread over her body, until every fiber of her being burned. She struggled to wake herself but couldn't pull her mind away from the images playing in her head. Her throat tightened. She tasted vomit. Its bitterness turned her stomach, producing more bile. She choked on it, but still, could not wake up.

"Hush," the voice said. "Let it do its job."

Let what do its job? A fever had taken hold of her body and it would kill her in the end. If she died, all of the shit she'd endured the past twenty-four hours would be for nothing. No one would know what was happening.

"Infection won't kill you. Let it in."

Infections were bad. She had to fight it.

"Rest. It'll be over soon."

Rachel resisted the tickling sensation in her brain. She was rewarded with a sharp, cold jolt at the base of her neck.

The parasite was reproducing. Multiplying inside her brain. She didn't know how she knew it, but supposed it was logical that she might sense such a thing. They'd seen the eggs, hadn't they? It was what parasites did. Feed off the host. Make babies. Spread to a new host. Now, it'd corrupt her neurological functions and convince her to kill herself so the larvae could escape and infect someone else.

She wouldn't allow it. It would end with her. She just had to figure out how to—

"It doesn't work like that," the voice said. "Just let it happen."

Let what happen?

Rachel saw Morris. He stood against a brilliant blue sky, smiling. His eyes seemed to hold hers, urging her to listen to the insanity the parasite caused her to imagine.

Then Morris was in bed. A white suit person stood over him, deadly glass vial in their hand. Rachel choked on a sob as she watched them inject Morris's arm with the contents. He lay still for several seconds. She watched as they checked his pulse, checked the glass bottle's label, and then checked his pulse again.

When the person in the white suit straightened, Morris opened his eyes and winked.

And finally, Rachel knew the voice came from somewhere real.

"See?" it said. "Let it in. Then you can go to him."

The voice no longer felt like insanity taking over. It comforted her as the pain in her head reached a crescendo. She thought her brain might explode but dying no longer scared her. Rachel now embraced the possibility of being free from it all. Above it. Beyond...

"Good girl."

* * *

"What have you done?" Catherine's fury almost choked the words. She had gone to the lab to gather Morris's files and the results from the most recent round of bloodwork taken by her team. When she returned, eleven people were dead. "We agreed to wait. Stop that."

"Died in their sleep," George's man told her. "Can't do much about that, ma'am."

"Fucking liars. I won't let you get away with this. We have laws in this country. Doesn't matter who you work for. You're not above the law."

"Look, I have my orders," the man said. "I did as I was told. Take it up with the boss."

"I will. Where is he?"

"Downstairs. In the lab."

"Don't you go anywhere either," she said. "You're all accountable for this."

"Yep."

Catherine walked away from the carnage, unable to watch the people who trusted her to make them well die by her team's hand. She had no doubt George made the medical staff administer the poison. Why get his hands dirty? If the CDC did the killing, then he could be certain everyone would keep their mouths shut

Her anger at George paled in comparison to the rage she felt at her stupidity. She should never have trusted him. During the short walk to the university, her anger burned so hot she could barely form a coherent thought. She hoped Rachel was smart enough to tell someone about the infection and the measures taken to contain it. Let the government try to explain murder away.

Men in black suits guarded the doors that opened into

the lobby of the main building, where Morris's room, and the research lab where located. They let her pass, but she heard one of them talking into his radio. "She's here," he said. "And she looks pissed."

She didn't hear the reply.

Morris's lab was located in the basement. She rode the elevator down, rehearsing the words she'd say when she faced George. How dare he do this without telling her. He said he cared about her. Respected her. Wouldn't proceed until she was on board. Should've trusted her instincts and... what? She couldn't research the parasite and guard the patients.

The doors opened. George stood, arms crossed in front of him, expectant smirk on his face. "Afternoon, Doctor Fairchild. I see you've been to quarantine ward."

"How dare you?"

"I told you I don't need your permission. The situation developed quickly, so I had no time to hold your hand. It had to be done."

"Why now? Why this second? You said I could—"

"No," George said, waving his arm toward the hallway. "You said you wanted to do more tests. I said if you could give me probable theories, I could give you forty-eight hours, but I promised nothing."

"That is not at all what you said."

"Come. Let me show you something."

She exited the elevator. "You can't distract me. This is murder. I won't be part of it."

"You already are. Trust me, your superiors are aware of what's happening. They agree it's for the best. Don't worry, dear. You won't be used as a patsy or whatever it is you're worried about."

She bit her lip to stop the reply that formed in her mind. Her superiors were all about politics. They left medicine behind long ago. If they approved George's actions, she'd already lost the fight. He would do whatever he pleased and fuck common sense. Screw right and wrong.

They approached Morris's room. The window had been replaced, but now had thin wires running over the glass. Inside, she saw him sitting on the edge of his bed, head down, bloody hands on his lap. Blood covered his chest and legs as well. It sprayed over the grey walls, across the white sheets, and pooled on the floor.

"Is that blood?"

George nodded. "Not his own."

"What happened?"

"Your team went in, as I instructed, and they gave him the injection."

"Let's not pretend this is something other than what it is. You mean they tried to kill him."

"Yes, as I ordered them to do. He was too far gone. You have to see that."

"How did the blood get there? Who did he hurt?"

"A young man who was only doing his job. One of yours. David, they tell me his name was."

"David Brown or David Johnson?"

"Why does it matter?"

She shrugged. "I don't know. I have to call his family."

"We'll take care of that."

"Why did Morris hurt him? How?"

"Well, we don't know the why, but I imagine it was instinctual. Just trying to survive. The video shows your guy, David, giving Morris the injection. When David checked his pulse, I think he realized Morris wasn't dead. He waited a minute, thinking, I imagine, that the meds might be taking a little longer than usual, and he checked Morris's pulse again. He turned toward the door, and then Morris opened his eyes."

"And what? Stabbed David?"

"I wish," George said. "David just... combusted."

"What? I don't understand."

George held up his hand. One of his men handed him a

tablet. George turned it on, swiped the screen a few times and then handed it to Catherine. "Watch."

She looked at the screen. It showed Morris sleeping. David entered the room. Injected Morris's arm with something. Morris was still, as George described. She couldn't see his face. The camera had been installed near the door, so it only showed a side view of what was happening. David walked toward the door, and then the camera went dark.

"That's his blood covering the lens," George said. "He literally just went poof." He made a gesture with his hands.

"Impossible."

He leaned over, closed the video file, and then touched an icon at the bottom of the screen. A gallery of photos appeared. A corpse, surrounded by blood. His torso was little more than shredded meat, ribs poking out, some intact, others fractured in half. She swiped. The next image showed the same body, this time, from the shoulders up.

"He was decapitated?"

George pointed to the window. "You'll find what remains of his head on the walls next to the door."

"Oh my God," she whispered. "This isn't possible. Morris isn't like this. He'd never—"

"And I told you they become something else. That isn't Morris in there."

"Why isn't he still killing then?"

"When they repaired the window, I had wires installed to electrify the room in the same manner we've electrified Charles's containment unit. Good thing, or he might have killed everyone in this place without leaving his hospital bed. As it is, my men charged in without thinking. No gear. Not even masks. Idiots. Now I'll probably have to euthanize them as well."

Poor baby. "Morris isn't violent. Maybe this wasn't even him. Are you sure Charles can't—"

"Positive. I told you, it changes everything about the

person it infects. They're no longer people, in my opinion."

"We still can't euthanize patients who aren't infected. It's one thing if they're dangerous, but healthy people who will never hurt anyone? I can't agree to that."

George took the tablet from her hands. He tucked it under her arm, and then gently guided her away from Morris's window. "And we won't lay a finger on healthy people."

"Forgive me if I don't believe you. I want to monitor this from now on. I'll let your people know who is a threat and who isn't."

"This is out of your hands now. I think it's time for you and your team to go home."

"I can't—"

"It's not a suggestion."

"We need to do autopsies. If we don't, we'll never find a cure for this thing."

"I'm not sure how many ways I have to say this, but you won't find a cure, Catherine. And I'm not interested in that anyway. My team will deal with the bodies and their autopsies. Every patient in quarantine is now the property of the United States government. We'll do what needs to be done. Protect and serve is our motto, after all."

She nodded, although his tone made her less than reassured. He sounded cold. Arrogant. Like he knew how this would go the whole time.

Like he hoped it would end like this...

"What about Morris?" she asked as the elevator doors opened.

"He's progressed too far for the usual methods. I'll take him back to our facility and then decide what we'll do with him."

"What does that mean?"

"A man with abilities like he might have could be very useful. Unlike Charles, he's still got some humanity left in him. I want to appeal to that side of him. Get him to help do some good in the world, instead of blowing people up with his mind."

"And if he refuses, like Charles did?"

"If he won't play ball, then he's no use to anyone."

"If you can't kill them, then what is there to do except lock him up for God knows how long, as you've done with Charles?"

George smiled, pushing her forward. "I didn't say they couldn't be killed."

"Yes, you did."

"Did I?"

She scowled.

"My mistake. They're difficult to kill, but not impossible. The first hurdle is to prevent them from getting inside your mind. Then, if one can get close enough to relieve them of their heads, they'll most assuredly die."

The doors closed. Catherine stared at her reflection in the smudged metal.

If they could get close enough. She pressed the "L" button. The elevator moved upward.

She believed Morris and Charles were threats to the welfare of healthy people, possibly even to themselves, but she didn't believe there was nothing to be done about them. They should be studied. The secrets their bodies might hold could be life altering for humanity. It could be life ending as well, she supposed. If they infected others, managed to spread the parasite worldwide, and their victims survived… she couldn't fathom a world where everyone lived forever. Earth's resources were depleted as it was. With a race of beings that endured for centuries consuming what remained, Earth would essentially die.

And then what?

The elevator chimed and the doors opened to reveal the lobby.

Maybe Charles didn't need to eat. Didn't need oxygen or anything that the "normal" human required. If that were the case, then it's possible their endangered resources would flourish because of this parasite. Earth might be saved from what had been inevitable until now.

She couldn't know, because George and his bosses were keeping him all to themselves.

Catherine walked to the main doors. As she exited the building, she nodded at George's guards. They didn't respond. She walked toward the parking lot. Behind her, she heard a radio squawk.

Her job was to protect people. Heal them. No way was she going to let George get away with this. She'd go to the reputable news agencies first. Her job wasn't important if the oath she'd taken meant nothing anymore. They couldn't arrest her for talking. She was a doctor. It was her duty to protect the public.

If the reputable agencies wouldn't share what she had to tell them, she'd take to the Internet. It'd be a matter of a leaked document, one she'd have to manufacture somehow, and then social media would do the legwork.

A strange sensation tickled her brain, urging her to walk faster. Catherine saw her car. Just a few feet to go. The tickling became a sharp pain. No. She wasn't infected. She'd followed every protocol.

"Dr. Fairchild?" a man called. "Wait."

Catherine took out her keys. George wouldn't hurt her, but something said she shouldn't turn. Just get in her car and go. The pain in her head intensified.

"Dr. Fairchild, please. You're in—"

* * *

"Can you hear me?"

Rachel sat on her bed, replaying the dream she'd just woke from. In it, she had a gun. It felt so warm in the dream, it was almost like she actually held it. Dr. Fairchild walked briskly toward a black car.

"Do it," Morris urged. "She'll tell the world about us, and we'll never be free."

In the dream, Rachel lifted the gun. Dr. Fairchild kept walking. Someone called her name. A man. Dr. Fairchild didn't stop, though. She walked faster.

"Now," Morris said.

Rachel had squeezed the trigger. The gun made no sound, but almost as soon as she fired, she dreamed she saw blood spray from Dr. Fairchild's head. Her body stood motionless, headless, for just a moment, before it disappeared.

Dr. Fairchild wasn't a bad person. Why would she think Morris would tell her to kill the poor woman? Why would Rachel oblige him, even if it were just a dream?

She woke slowly. It was dark. Had she slept through the night and day? More than a day? She wasn't sure. It felt like she'd slept for a week.

"Rachel."

The voice clung to her mind, but it wasn't real. She just had to ignore it. The parasite was still tormenting her. If she could just be stronger than the urges…

A sour odor tormented her nose. Rachel sat up. A yellow crust coated her shirt and the bedsheets. It contained bits of white and brown. The roast beef sandwich she'd inhaled before arriving at the hotel. So, she had puked. She stood. The room tilted a bit but righted itself as she walked carefully toward the bathroom. She removed her soiled shirt and then her pants. A shower and then she'd figure out what to do. Check on the doctor, maybe. Make sure her dream was just a dream.

How could it be anything else?

"Why won't you listen to me?"

Because you're not real.

She turned on the water. Stepped inside the tub. The hot spray felt nice. Cleaned the cobwebs from her mind. Rachel relaxed and enjoyed the sensation of her taut muscles unknotting. She felt human again. For now.

"Rachel. It's me. Seriously."

Morris's voice hadn't left her when the dream ended. Despite her best efforts to make it stop, it pushed into her head. Invaded her thoughts.

"No," she said aloud. Her own voice startled her. It was deeper. Too loud.

"Don't ignore me."

She soaped up her hair, rinsed, and then did the same to her body.

"Rachel, just tell me if you can hear me."

Maybe if she acknowledged it, her mind would let it go. She sighed. "Yes," she whispered. "I can hear you."

"How is your head?"

"Fine."

"And how do you feel?"

She opened her eyes. The room was dark. Why hadn't she turned on the light? Probably because she saw every detail within the room, right down to the dirt in the grout lines of the tiled walls of the shower, as clearly as if she'd put everything under a bright spotlight. Strange. "I feel okay. Weird, but not in a bad way."

"Good. It's time."

"For what?"

"He's waiting for us."

"Who?"

"You did the right thing. She was going to tell them about us."

Rachel frowned. Her imagination had gone and lost its shit. She couldn't even hallucinate in a logical manner anymore. "I'm confused, Mo."

"We have to hide. It's the only way."

"Hide from who?"

"Everyone."

"Who is waiting for us?"

Silence.

"Mo?" Why was she so scared that an imaginary voice might have left? She should be happy. She wanted him gone, didn't she? But the sound of his voice, so familiar and real, made her feel safe. She didn't realize it until it disappeared. "Mo, talk to me."

"They're coming. Wait outside for me. Okay?"

"Outside where?"

"The hospital. Promise you'll be there."

She didn't want to go back there. Couldn't. It wasn't safe.

"Rachel, you can do this."

"I can't." She turned off the water. Grabbed the towel hanging next to the tub. "I don't understand any of this. Don't know what's real anymore."

"I'm real. This is real. If you don't do this, I'll die like the others. Then they'll come after you. The only way out of this is together. Understand?"

She nodded. What harm was there in going to the hospital? He'd either show, proving this was real, or he wouldn't, confirming she was hallucinating. Either way, she'd have answers. "Okay. I'll be there."

"Good. Go."

Rachel dried herself off. She left the bathroom, picked up the shopping bag containing a clean shirt and slowly dressed. She moved instinctively, not thinking about her actions before she did them. Her body reacted on its own. Autopilot.

She picked up her backpack of money, walked to the door, and then opened it. Outside, the air was heavy. It'd rain soon. She inhaled deeply, savoring the sensation of breathing through her nose without pain. Thank God those headaches were gone. Maybe she hadn't been infected at all. A cluster of migraines, even if she had never experienced one before, could just be a cluster of migraines.

Doesn't explain the blood, though, or how she ended up in that alley with no recollection of what happened at her cousin's house. She still had no idea where she was or what she did during the days she'd blacked out.

She pushed the thought from her mind. Her subconscious wanted her to go to the hospital, so she'd go. As long as she didn't get too close and they didn't find her, it'd be fine. She could confirm Morris was okay, and then decide how to proceed.

"You'll have to kill them all, dear," the voice said. This one wasn't Morris. It was the one she'd heard the day she left the hospital. She didn't trust it.

"No." Her legs carried her to the car she'd stolen despite her refusal to do as the voice said.

"It's us or them."

"Who is us?"

"Me, you, and your friend."

"Morris?"

"Yes. I'll tell you what to do."

Rachel opened the car door and then tossed her backpack inside. "I'm not killing anyone."

"Listen closely. One wrong move and everything we've worked toward will fall apart."

"And I'll die?"

"Yes. Are you ready?"

Rachel sat in the driver's seat. "Go ahead."

"First, get on the chopper."

CHAPTER 17

Rachel waited all night in the parking lot, trying to figure out how to get inside and to the roof without being seen. Finally, as the sun made its way over the horizon, she heard the helicopter. The voice in her head told her she could alter a person's thoughts. When she voiced her doubts, he promised to help her.

"Think about what you want them to do. I'll do the rest," he said.

So, she'd walked past the guards, smiling at one, silently urging him to stand down as she passed. He smiled back. Had she really just manipulated another person's mind? No way.

She tried again with the guard at the elevator. "I'm not a threat. You want to help me," she thought.

The guard nodded as she pushed the button. "Need help?"

"How do I get to the roof?"

He stared.

"I need to get to the roof," she pushed.

"Yes," the voice said. "Help the poor woman."

"You'll need a key card," he said, reaching into his pocket. "Here. Use mine."

"Thanks," she took the card and then got in the elevator. "Oh, and you didn't see me."

"Didn't see you," he agreed.

Rachel almost grinned as the doors closed.

On the roof, the helicopter waited. She searched for somewhere to hide.

"You don't need to hide," the voice said. "Tell them to let you on."

Preparing herself for the worst, Rachel walked toward the helicopter. The pilot got out and raised his hand as she approached. "Sorry," he'd said. "You need authorization to be up here."

"I have authorization," she said. "Let me get in."

"She's harmless," the voice said. "Just needs a ride."

"Where you going?"

"With you," Rachel said. "But it has to be a secret."

He rubbed his chin. "Boss won't like a stowaway."

"We won't tell if you won't," the voice said.

The pilot glanced over his shoulder and then took Rachel's arm. "Okay. But get behind the seats, under the tarp. Don't make a sound."

"Thank you so much."

"Yes," the voice said. "Maybe you'll survive this."

The pilot laughed. "I sure hope so."

And that was it. He walked away. When he returned less than an hour later, he didn't look in Rachel's direction. Didn't let on that he remembered her being there at all.

This was nuts.

"Not nuts," the voice said. "Not even magic."

"Then how is it possible?"

"Evolution."

"We're infected, not evolved."

"I guess it depends on one's point of view. Now hush. He's coming."

* * *

Morris could hear their thoughts. He didn't understand how or why, but he stopped questioning what was happening to him. Once the headaches passed, everything took on a new clarity and focus. He now knew the voice in his head belonged to a man named Charles, and that Charles knew far more about the parasite than anyone. He'd have answers no one else could provide and would know what to do about it.

While he accepted his newfound abilities, Morris had still been shocked when Rachel's thoughts drifted into his mind. The poor girl was terrified. He felt her fear as though it were his own. She'd have to suck it up, though. The situation was life and death, both his and hers.

He did as Charles instructed and tried to reach out to Rachel. When she finally answered, it stunned him enough that he didn't know what else to say. Charles whispered a few words, and then Rachel replied to him as well. Morris gave her the reassurance she needed and then Charles took over and the connection was lost.

As the G-men readied themselves for a trip, Morris quietly listened to their conversations, both internal and with each other. George, the leader, received a phone call not long ago. Dr. Fairchild was dead. Morris knew this already, but hearing it confirmed sent goosebumps over his skin. He and Rachel had done that.

With nothing but their minds.

It was unfathomable. Impossible.

Rachel believed it was a dream, but it happened. Morris was as sure of it as he was of his own name. They'd killed someone. He'd killed more than that, although, he reasoned, he couldn't really be blamed for doing something he had no knowledge of being able to do. That wasn't his fault. George should've said something. Warned someone. Their blood was on George's hands, not his.

Morris also knew that George was... excited, although he didn't let his men know it. He didn't fear Morris, although he should, given what Morris had done. Maybe he believed the electrical current surrounding the hospital room blocked Morris's abilities. Where he got such an idea, Morris wasn't sure, but it was wrong. Charles instructed him to play along. Let them believe he was helpless as long as they had him wired up.

"Do nothing," Charles had said. "Let them put you on the helicopter. They'll bring you to me and then we can make our escape."

The door to his room opened. Several men with large guns walked in. George followed. Morris remained seated on the edge of his bed.

"Hands," George said.

Morris lifted his arms. The men didn't move right away. He could taste their fear, despite the weapons that ensured Morris couldn't hurt more than one of them before the rest opened fire and stopped him forever.

"Reassure them," Charles ordered.

"Do it," Morris said. "Please. I don't want to hurt anyone else."

"We'll help you," George said. A lie. "Just no more funny business. Don't think about trying anything, or we'll put a bullet in your brain. Got it?"

Morris nodded. Charles assured him the only they could kill him was to sever the connection between his body and his brain. A bullet could do that, he knew, so he just wouldn't give them the reason or the opportunity to do that.

"Wire him up," George ordered. "Come on. We don't have all day."

Two men approached Morris, holding out a white jacket covered in wires and probes. A third followed with a hat-like object, also covered with wires.

"What's this?" Morris asked.

"We can't help you if a single thought could mean our demise," George explained. "This is for our safety and yours. It won't hurt."

Morris let them put the jacket on him and then the hat. He waited as they connected the leads to two battery packs, which had been sewn into the back of the jacket. They pressed a button on the battery packs and a jolt rippled over his body. George was right. It didn't hurt. It didn't feel good either, though.

"Okay," George said. "Let's get him out of here."

They helped Morris stand. His legs were fine, but he pretended to stumble, and they lifted him, making it unnecessary for him to walk at all. As they led him to the elevator, Morris considered getting rid of them all before they reached the lobby. Then he could run, find Rachel and—

"No," Charles said. "You must come to me. Do not harm them yet."

"But they're going to use me as a guinea pig," Morris thought. "You too."

"They only think they'll do that. I haven't played along all these years, waited to find more like me, just to lose the opportunity to be free because you're afraid of a few pokes and jabs."

"What if I can't get us out?"

"Let me worry about that."

Morris nodded. They were on the roof now. George led the way to a helicopter. As they walked toward it, Morris breathed deeply. He lifted his face toward the sun, soaking in its warmth.

"Enjoy it," the man on his left said. "Where you're going, there won't be any sunshine for a long time."

Morris didn't reply. He let them help him into the helicopter. George was already strapped in. They secured him into his own seat and then one guard got in beside him. The rest remained on the roof.

He sensed someone nearby.

"Rachel?" he called silently. "You here?"

"Yes," she replied. "Behind you."

He didn't turn. Smiling, Morris closed his eyes as the chopper lifted.

* * *

No one in the helicopter spoke until they approached a large structure built into the base of a mountain. The pilot said something, probably radioing whoever was on the ground, and the man in the black suit cleared his throat.

"You didn't have to kill her, you know."

"Kill who?" Morris asked.

"Catherine. She wouldn't have told anyone about you. I'd have made sure of it."

Morris laughed. "I didn't kill her. Actually, I heard she spontaneously combusted."

"You're a scientist. Don't tell me you believe that nonsense."

"Spontaneous combustion is a real thing. We haven't explained it, but we accept that it's possible."

"Her head didn't explode on its own. That's a trick Charles is fond of. The only thing I don't know is how you knew to do the same thing. It took him decades to grasp what he could do."

Rachel tried to pry into the man's mind, as the voice said she could do, but she couldn't break in. Maybe the voice was wrong.

"You won't get anything from George," the voice said. "It's best to stay out of his thoughts anyway. Nothing good in there."

Rachel worried over that. Why couldn't they hear his thoughts? If the voice was real, and telling the truth, then she and Morris could hear anyone. Influence anyone. She could hear the pilot and had heard the soldiers posted at the hospital. Why was this man different?

She got no answers from the voice as the helicopter landed. Rachel waited for a message, but none came.

"I didn't kill her," Morris said as the man helped him from his seat.

"Who?"

"Catherine. That wasn't me."

"Who then?"

"Charles did it."

The man paused, startled by the mention of Charles.

"How do you... never mind. Catherine obviously mentioned him to you or you pulled it from her head. What you don't realize is, he can't use his abilities. I've blocked them."

Another laugh. "Like you've blocked mine?"

Rachel heard something outside the helicopter, but it was muffled.

"Shit," the pilot whispered. "Sir—"

"Christ," George yelled. "Enough!"

"Get these cuffs off me," Morris said.

Silence.

"Don't make me hurt you too."

A sigh.

"Get out of the chopper," Morris instructed. "Now."

"Fine. Okay."

Shuffling. Grunts.

"You can come out, Rachel," Morris said.

Rachel happily crawled from her hiding spot. Blood covered the windshield of the helicopter. The pilot still sat in his seat, chest ripped wide open. "You didn't have to do that, Mo. We can make them do what we want."

Morris took off a ridiculous helmet covered with wires and lights. "I didn't do it. *He* did."

"Who?" George asked.

"The man who can't use his abilities, because you've blocked them."

As Rachel exited the helicopter, Morris shoved George toward the doors of the facility. She followed them slowly, her eyes riveted to the carnage on the ground. At least a dozen bodies scattered across the patches of grass and dirt. Some without heads, others with no external damage at all.

"Rachel!"

She jogged the last several feet to the doors. "Why are we doing this? We don't need to kill every—"

"I told you, it wasn't me. He's waiting."

"Listen," George said. "We can make a deal. This isn't you, Morris. You're not a killer."

"I know. Let us in, please."

George pressed the keypad. The doors opened.

"But *he* is a killer," a voice, Charles, said inside Rachel's mind. "Don't trust him."

"Why not just kill him too?" she wondered.

"Because I want him to set me free."

Rachel looked at Morris. He nodded.

"Charles wants to turn the entire world into what you two have become," George said. "Only a small percentage will survive, though. We've run the numbers. Looked at what we know and figured out all the possibilities. While it would be wonderful to evolve into a race of superior beings who don't get ill or age, if you infect the world, you'll reduce the population to a fraction of what it is. There's no evidence what's left would be able to reproduce either. It'll be... a genocide. And for what? A few thousand new and improved humans that can't have children?"

Rachel didn't want to hurt anyone. She just wanted to survive this. To be left alone. She followed them to an elevator. Morris looked angry, but he said nothing.

"He's insane," George continued as the doors closed. "Left alone too long with far too much power. He lost his humanity years ago, but you two haven't yet. There's still time to do the right thing. Imagine what we could do if we understood what the parasite has done to you. We could study it, figure out how to harness the good parts of it so that everyone benefits, rather than killing anyone not strong enough to get to the other side."

"Shut up," Morris said. "We're taking Charles. If you don't fight, then you can live."

"He won't let me live." George pressed a button at the base of the keypad and the elevator moved downward. "He won't let a single person on this base survive."

"They don't deserve life," Charles said. "You know what they're capable of. What they've already done."

Rachel was conflicted. She knew what George had done.

He killed dozens of innocent people, both infected and healthy, just because he feared this parasite. If he lived, he'd be gunning for them as long as he had the power to do so. She couldn't live with an axe over her head. On the other hand, she was developing a mistrust of Charles and his motives. He helped her find Morris, yes, but at what cost? Why did he want them at all? He stood a better chance at disappearing if he was alone.

"What if we left him here?" Rachel asked. "He's dangerous, Mo. Surely, you can sense that."

"He knows things we don't," Morris said as the elevator doors opened. "Understands the infection. He might even know how to cure it."

"Is that what he told you?" George asked and then laughed. "He's lying. The only cure for this infection is death. You don't think I've looked into it?"

"Like..." Rachel couldn't finish the sentence.

"Decapitation," George finished. "Bullet to the brain. Knife through the skull. That's the only way you'll be free of the parasite growing in every cell of your body."

"Sir?" a man standing next to the door said.

Rachel hadn't noticed him; he'd stood so still in the shadows.

"You're no longer needed," George said. "Get out of here."

"But that's against protocol." The man raised his gun. "Are you hurt, sir?"

"No. Just go. You're relieved of duty."

"Do as the man said," Morris instructed. "We don't want to hurt you."

The man looked uncertain. He didn't lower his weapon, but he didn't advance either.

"They're like Charles," George explained. "You can't fight them. Just go. Evacuate the facility. I'll be fine."

"Sir, I can't—" his words turned into a choking sound.

Rachel covered her mouth as his head turned violently

to the left. She heard the bones of his neck breaking a second before he crumpled to the floor.

"Open the door," Morris said. "And stop filling her head with lies."

George leaned forward, stared into a small screen on the wall, and the door clicked. "I'm not lying. I guess you'll have to see that for yourself. By the way," he pointed to the dead man on the floor, "was that you or Charles?"

"Does it matter?"

"I suppose not. Simply curious."

They entered a large room. While not wide, it was long. At the far end, a glass and steel box took up the majority of the wall. Morris led them toward it. Rachel still had an unsettled feeling about it all. Why did she suddenly fear this Charles person?

"Don't be afraid," he said. "I'd never hurt you."

She didn't believe him.

As they reached the middle, they saw a man standing in what looked like a bedroom. He looked like a younger, better-looking version of George, and smiled when they stopped in front of him.

"Let him out," Morris said.

"That requires the assistance of the man you just killed."

"Convenient."

George sighed. "Charles knows the protocols in place. Tell them, Charles."

Charles placed a hand on the glass. "I've also seen you override every one of them. I have faith in you, son."

George's cheeks pinkened. He didn't move to open the locks on the prison Charles was stuck in, though. "If I let you out, you'll kill me. If I don't, you have to keep me alive, because no one else can set you free. I think the wisest course of action for me is to do nothing."

Charles laughed. Rachel was startled by the sound. It seemed unnatural. Too cold.

"What now?" Morris asked. "Is he really the only one

who can let you out?"

Charles shrugged. "He'll come around."

"We could just push on his mind, like you showed me," Rachel suggested, although the last thing she wanted was to let this creature loose on the world. "Make him want to unlock the door."

"Ah," Charles said. "An interesting idea, except old George here has ensured I can't do that to him."

"How?"

"Tell them, George."

"I don't know what you're talking about."

"Oh, that's right. You don't remember, because I told you to forget."

Rachel stared at both men. George looked confused and frightened. Charles looked smug. "What's going on?"

Charles traced a line over the glass. "George infected himself. I told him it was the only way to protect his mind and his life from me, should I ever escape and seek retribution for the horrors I've endured here."

"You're lying," George said. "I'd never do that."

"No?"

"No."

"I didn't kill the guard, Georgie. That was you."

"I did not."

Rachel glanced at Morris. He glared at both men.

"I should have put a thought in there before you changed, so you'd remember when I gave the right word. Oh, wait..." Charles grinned. "I did."

"I won't let you out. Spin whatever tales you want."

"Grapefruit."

"Pardon?"

Rachel saw the confusion in George's eyes. It lasted only a moment. Then, slowly, his face changed. His eyes widened, his jaw clamped shut. For a moment, his face was so red, Rachel was certain his head would explode like Catherine's had, but the color slowly drained away.

"You son of a bitch," George whispered.

"Not a nice thing to say about my mother, Georgie."

"I'd remember being infected. You can't—"

"And yet, here we are. Problem is, only certain types of people survive and gain abilities. There's no way to predict, as George knows, thanks to his many studies. Some survive but gain little more than improved health and longevity. No psychic abilities. The theory was that people from the same gene pool would develop similar traits. Right, George?"

"We have the same DNA," George said. "So, it would make sense that I'd have the same abilities as you have."

"True."

George frowned.

"Wait," Rachel said. "You two are related?"

"Charles is my great grandfather."

She swallowed that information slowly. "That means he's more than a hundred years old."

"Much more," Charles said. "I age well, yes?"

"But that's not possible."

"With alien DNA in your body, anything is possible," George said. "And he's not lying. He lived near the Baker plantation when something crashed in a field nearby. No one realized he'd been infected until much later. We never recovered the object that crashed, but we found the parasite in the soil."

"Or rather," Charles said. "It found you. You euthanized an entire team just to stop it. Tragic."

"That was before my time."

"But you are just as guilty as your predecessors."

"I'd know if I had abilities," George said. "I'd remember being infected. You put these memories in my head to fuck with me."

"Did I?"

"Why would you want me to be like you? I thought you hated me."

"I could never hate you. Sure, you're misguided and a

little slow, but you're the only family I have left. Maybe I'm a sentimental old fool, but that means something to me."

"I may be slow, but I'm not stupid. It's kind of hard not to notice something like the ability to read minds."

"You've used your powers, but you never knew they were there, so you had no idea it was you at the time."

"That's ridiculous. I'd know."

"Try to move something."

"No."

"Come on, Georgie. Humor me."

"Just do it," Morris said. "So we can get the hell out of here."

"This is stupid," George said, but turned his eyes from Charles. He stared for a long time, and then the bed moved a couple of inches. "No. You did that."

"You did it. I knew you'd never set me free unless you had good reason to do so. While I didn't want to show my hand by shattering the walls you've built around me, I can reach out psychically, and have many times."

"The electricity doesn't work?"

Charles laughed. "No, son. It never worked."

"Why did you pretend?"

"I decided my best strategy was to make you feel safe. Let you believe I was harmless inside your little electrical field. Then, I worked on your mind. You were a tough nut to crack, though. Must be your stellar genetics."

"I'd remember infection," George insisted. "It doesn't make sense that you'd give me the same abilities."

"Doesn't it? I needed allies, Georgie, to achieve my goals. So, when the call came about my old neighbors being dug up, I saw a perfect opportunity. You, being of my blood, were almost guaranteed to survive the infection, so I pushed at you hard. You folded, eventually, and booked your little holiday. Remember that?"

"I…"

"Then I told you that you'd forget everything that

happened on that holiday. You'd only remember leaving the facility and returning. In that empty space, you exposed yourself to the parasite, became infected, and locked yourself away until the adjustment period was over."

"Is this true?" Rachel asked.

"It can't be."

She could see the terror on George's face. He recalled some of it, obviously.

"You're one of us now," Charles said. "And if anything happens to me, your superiors will know everything. Think you can survive on your own?"

Chapter 18

Morris helped George drag the guard's body to the enclosure. He sensed Rachel's anxiety. Willed her to calm down more than once. She didn't. Her mistrust had infected him. It boiled at the pit of his stomach. Charles had answers. He knew this parasite inside and out. He'd helped them survive. Why shouldn't they trust him? George is the one who lied and murdered people. Charles just did what was necessary to be free.

Why did he feel like Charles was the devil then, and not George? Morris actually pitied George. Like himself and Rachel, George had been infected unwillingly. He'd been forced to be like this, just as they had.

George punched a series of numbers into the keypad next to the enclosure. He then leaned forward, looked into a tiny square, and then hauled the guard to his knees. "Help me."

Morris lifted the guard's head while George put his face to the square. He held the man's eye open, waited, and then the panel beeped. Morris heard something click.

Rachel walked toward him as the glass at the center of the enclosure made a whooshing sound. Charles walked out, smiling.

"Wait," Rachel said. "If you could shatter this at any time, why'd you make them do all that?"

"Shits and giggles?"

She scowled.

"Come now, love," Charles chided. "I've had literally

nothing to do for decades. Allow me to have a bit of fun."

Morris recognized the set of her shoulders, the way her chin jutted forward. Charles pissed her off. Before she could anger the only person who knew anything about what they were and how they should proceed, Morris put his hand on her back.

She looked up at him. "What?"

"It's okay. We're safe."

"Keep fooling yourselves," George muttered. "Maybe we'll all live happily ever after too."

"Enough of this childishness," Charles said. "We have to prepare."

"For what?" Morris asked.

"Evolution." He tapped his chin. "That's kind of boring too, isn't it? We need to strive for something more interesting. How about world domination? I think that has an exciting ring to it."

"You're insane," Rachel said.

"Oh, I assure you, I'm not. Socially awkward, possibly, because I've been bored to tears by my own company for longer than you've been alive, but I'm not crazy."

"I won't infect people."

"You can't, I'm afraid. Neither can I. The parasite is transmittable by air, but not once it has integrated with its host. Perhaps if we were to die, and our insides were exposed, it might be able to find a new host, but not as we are now. Sadly, Georgie killed our potential vectors at the hospital. By now, I imagine his team has cremated every last one, and their ashes are somewhere deep and dark."

"The burial site—"

"Alas, George and his goons poured chemicals and concrete over the only other resource available. I've had to revise my infection plan, which was probably a stupid one anyway. Imagine, a world of people just like us. We'd never get them to do what we want, because we'd have no leverage. I'd rather be the most powerful person in the room. Wouldn't you?"

"Then how are we helping anyone evolve into whatever we are?"

"George has ensured there is a way to infect, should we need it. For now, though, we're not infecting anyone else."

Morris didn't voice his confusion. If they couldn't infect anyone, then what did Charles have planned? He was afraid to ask. George, however, was not.

"What are you going to do?" he asked.

"*We*," Charles said. "Are going to reshape the world, beginning with this country."

"How?"

"Well, Georgie, you're going to run for president. Don't worry, I'll manage your campaign. With me by your side, you can't lose."

"What will that achieve?" Morris asked.

Charles stretched, and then walked toward the lab on the other side of the room. "First, we'll reform healthcare in this country. It's long past time to adopt a free system anyway. We'll use it to weed out the bad apples. Keep the genetically superior, of course, and then, we'll start working on the economic nightmare that the social class system has become. I can't believe it's endured so long, to be honest."

"Communism has been tried and it failed," George said.

Charles snorted. "I'm not turning the world into a communist utopia, son. God, that'd be so dull."

"Then how would you eliminate social classes?"

"I wouldn't. I'd manipulate them. The rich and powerful will be my puppets. The poor would be... I'm not sure yet. Maybe we'd just get rid of them. They're a drain on the economy and our limited resources. I suppose they have their uses, ensure the rich stay that way, so getting rid of them all is shortsighted. Why don't we revisit that one later? I need to think on it."

Morris was trapped in a novel. A bad one that hadn't even been plotted to the end. He shook his head. "You can't do that. No one will allow it."

"Oh, they will, because I'll tell them to. People will do whatever I want. In time, they'll do whatever you want as well. Not yet, as you're not at full capacity, but eventually. Now, I've been practicing for years, so my powers are limitless. That's my theory anyway. Got a few soldiers of my own already. I'm not sure how far my abilities extend, but I do know I'm able to hear thoughts from anyone on this continent. That means I can manipulate those minds as well. I imagine, in time, you three will be able to do the same. You're practically infants at the moment, though, so I'll have to run the show for now."

"I won't do this," George said.

Charles laughed. "You will or you'll die. I'll give you the night to sleep on it. Let's clean up and then we'll all retire."

* * *

Charles made them sleep in the bunker beneath the facility, after cleaning up the bodies that littered the grounds outside. He knew about the drones that flew overhead every eight hours. Knew anything suspicious would send an alert to the Pentagon, which would mean security protocols would be initiated, resulting in either total destruction of the facility, or a team of soldiers running to their deaths.

George did the scheduled check ins, which assured whoever was listening that the facility was secure, but not because he feared what Charles would do to him if he didn't. He feared what Charles would do to the team sent to check on the facility if his superiors didn't hear from them. He hated this game of chicken, but the best thing for him to do, for now anyway, was to lay low. Be agreeable. Wait for the opportunity to do something, while ensuring no one else got hurt.

"Can he hear our thoughts?" Rachel whispered.

"I don't think so," George said. "But I'm not sure. Maybe

sometimes?"

"He's nuts," she said. "We can't infiltrate the government or whatever he's thinking. He can control minds, but not all of them at once. The sheer amount of will and energy that would require is... well, it's immeasurable, I imagine, and I don't think anyone here has what it takes."

"Not even Charles?"

"No. Not even him."

"I agree. Some people aren't suggestible. We ran tests. Not everyone is susceptible to his abilities, so at some point he'll cross someone he can't manipulate. He'd just kill them or make one of us do it. Put someone he can control in their place." George rubbed the stubble on his chin. "What he's proposing is possible, though, if he got enough people past initial stages of infection, and then put them in positions of power. No mind control needed once they call the shots, right?"

"Yeah, but it's a terrible idea. He'd destroy this country."

"That I definitely agree with. Whatever he has planned, it's going to end in death for a lot of people. I don't think he cares about that. The parasite has stolen whatever humanity he had."

"He did care enough to leave his wife and children, to spare them from infection."

"Because he thought they'd kill him. It was self-serving, not an act of kindness."

She shook her head. "I don't believe it was entirely selfish. He cared once. Maybe if we reminded him of how he used to be, or maybe made him remember his kids—"

"Been there, done that," he said. "The Charles that got infected all those years ago is not the same Charles we're dealing with. We'll be just like him eventually."

"I refuse to believe that. We can still do good."

"You're adorable."

"Am I?" She looked at him, eyebrows raised, face flushed. "Since you have all the answers, tell me, what are we going to do? Are you even going to try to stop him?"

George watched Charles, who sat on the opposite side of the room, explaining something to Morris, who had enough sense to look terrified. He often glanced at Rachel, but he said nothing. Did nothing. Just listened to whatever garbage Charles filled his head with. Whatever happened, George doubted they'd get much help from Morris.

"We can't let him just murder people," Rachel said. "I know he said we can't infect, but I don't believe him."

"He's not lying about that. We tested his blood. Ran trials to try to recreate the infection so we could figure out how to kill the parasite. He can't infect."

"Does he have soil from the site? Blood from the patients you killed?"

George cringed. He had killed innocent people, but it was necessary. They'd have an end of the world scenario happening if he hadn't. But then, they had one now anyway, so his efforts were wasted. "I don't know," he said to Rachel. "I guess he could've had someone gather those things."

"Could have?" She laughed. "You know he did. And when he talked about superior genetics, he was talking about killing anyone who didn't fit the bill as a host, so he must plan to infect people somehow."

"Yes," George admitted. He suspected Charles planned to infect more people, but not the way Rachel imagined. Better to take two infected people and breed, see what happens to the offspring. No guess work on the incubation period and survival odds of the host. The baby would have what's needed to support the parasite at conception. Man, he wished they'd had a female host years ago. At least then he'd know if such a thing were possible. Rachel didn't need to know that, though. She was the only female they had, and it wouldn't take long for her to do the math on what that meant. He smiled. "We can't do much about Charles at the moment, I'm afraid. I don't know how to kill him without a weapon."

Rachel glanced at Charles and then George felt

something touch his leg. He looked down.

"I took it off a body when we ran in," she said, tucking the gun back into her pants. "I don't know why. Instinct, I guess."

"Maybe Charles made you do it. He loves playing head games."

"It wasn't him. He trusts me."

"He trusts no one. What are you going to do with that anyway?"

She shook her head. "I don't know. Kill him?"

He laughed. "How?"

"Shoot him in the head?"

"Head shots look easy on television," George warned, "but a real target is totally different. You need skill. Accuracy. Have you ever fired a gun before?"

"Not in real life."

"Just...put it away. Don't do anything stupid."

"We can't let him leave here," she said. "I don't know how I know, but everything in me says if he gets out, it's all over for everyone. Including us."

"If we kill him, the government will know what we are and what he's made us do. He doesn't make idle threats, dear. When he said he put safeguards in place, he wasn't lying. I'm not sure how, but he's made sure that we're fucked if he dies, so even if we kill him, it'd still be over for us."

"I'll do what I have to for the greater good."

"Including sacrificing your freedom?"

"He's going to kill thousands of people."

"You're still suffering hallucinations," Charles said. "The effects of the initial stages tend to linger for a while. You can't trust your instincts now."

George sat up straight. "She's just talking."

"I know." Charles walked toward them. "And she doesn't know me. I understand her mistrust. What must happen *will* happen, love, with or without your help. In a day or two, the effects of infection will fade, and you'll see that."

"I'm scared," Rachel said. "And your plan has a lot of holes."

George thought she was convincing. Her tone held the right amount of fear. He eyed Charles, who seemed unconcerned about Rachel's intentions. He didn't take the gun. Didn't ask her why she had it. Instead, he brushed her bangs from her forehead, leaned down, kissed her gently, and then patted her cheek.

"Get some rest. You've had a rough couple of days."

She nodded. "I will. Thanks."

"In the morning, we'll sit down and figure out how to proceed. You're right. My plan isn't perfect. First step is ensuring there are no more like us out there. If there are, we'll have to gather them up. Make sure they're on our side."

"If they're not?"

"Off with their heads, as the saying goes."

Charles laughed at his joke. Rachel did not.

George knew there were no others. He'd been thorough when it came to that. He said nothing, though. The longer Charles spent preparing and covering his own ass, the better the odds they'd find a way to stop him. He wished he'd thought to take someone's gun. Could take Rachel's.

She looked at him before he'd finished the thought. Did she...? No. She was newly infected. Her abilities would be fresh. Weak. Charles described years of evolution before becoming what he was now. She probably couldn't do half of what Charles could. Of course, that would only be true if Charles's information were true. It was possible he lied... or he didn't know as much as they thought he did.

She smiled and then crossed the room to the bunks installed next to the door. Climbing to the top one, she laid down and then stared at George.

He looked away.

Four superhumans meant trouble. Charles was bad news on his own, but what happened when the rest of them lost all sense of right and wrong? Power did that to people.

George had training. He had integrity. They were loose cannons. Wild cards. While he was confident he could resist the urge to become an egomaniacal supervillain, he wasn't sure about Morris and Rachel. If they couldn't resist, Charles would get what he wanted. Maybe he'd have to kill all three of them. It was the only way to ensure the safety of humanity in general, and to prevent anyone from knowing what he'd become. He'd be locked up for sure. If it were him in his superiors' position, he'd put himself in a hole somewhere dark and toss the key.

He heard Rachel laugh.

"I'm on your side," she whispered. "Me and Morris just want this to be over."

George wanted to believe her. He looked at the bunks again. She'd closed her eyes. Morris and Charles resumed their discussion. Neither looked his way.

He closed his eyes and tried to reach Rachel the way he'd seen Charles do. She didn't answer, but he sensed her agreement somehow. When a pounding began behind his eyes, he stopped. The pain was almost bad enough to make him vomit.

Charles said he'd changed, so why the headache?

"My bad," Rachel whispered. "Just testing things out."

CHAPTER 19

"We have to," Rachel said. "It's the only way."

Morris knew she was right. They'd spent two days at the facility, while Charles prepared for "world domination." During those two days, he realized the man was certifiable. While he might have been human at some point, his ability to empathize, to think rationally, disappeared in the very long time he'd spent in George's cell. He was narcissistic, cold and without conscience. Such a man, given his abilities, was dangerous.

Too dangerous to be set free.

"How, though?" Morris asked. He continued putting the plastic vials of liquid into a bag, as they whispered. He didn't know what was in them. Didn't really care. Charles had instructed them to pack up everything in the lab. "He knows every thought before we think it."

"No, he doesn't." Rachel zipped the bag she'd packed and picked up another. "We're letting him in. If you can build a wall, metaphorically, he can't get inside your head."

"That only works in the movies, Rachel."

"Seriously. I've tested it. Try to read my mind."

Morris sighed. He reached out to Rachel, but instead of feeling the soft darkness of her mind, he felt something hard push back.

"See?" she said. "I imagine a sheet of steel every time he's around, and keep that at the back of my mind, no matter what I'm thinking or doing. It works."

He wished he could believe that. More likely, Charles

was playing with her. He loved games. "Let's say you're right and he has no idea what we're thinking. How are we going to kill him?"

"Bullet to the brain."

Morris laughed. "And after? Do you think George will let us live? We're no match for either of them. You're a student and I'm a scientist. Hardly battle ready."

"We don't need to be," she said. "George won't hurt us. If we leave and never come back, he'll just go on as he did before."

"I doubt that."

She smiled. "We know his darkest secret. He'll do what we say, because if he doesn't, we'll tell everyone what he is."

"That's assuming he lets us live long enough to make demands."

"Let's worry about one threat at a time. Charles first."

"Just drop it," Morris said. "Please."

"I can't."

He sighed but said no more. As they filled the backpacks, he tried to get into her head. The wall still stood. He hoped she was right about Charles. He'd hate to see her harmed because of youthful ignorance.

"Don't worry about her," he heard Charles's voice and paused in his packing. "Everything is going according to plan."

Morris glanced at Rachel. She seemed oblivious to Charles's presence. "She's impulsive," he thought. "But she would never hurt anyone."

"She already has."

Right. Catherine. Morris licked his lips. "I'll keep her in line. She won't do anything if I refuse to back her up."

"No need," Charles replied. "Let her do as she must."

Morris wasn't sure what game Charles was playing, but he didn't want to be part of it. He just wanted to leave the facility and get back to his life. No one had to know what he was. Now that he knew he couldn't pass the parasite to anyone, it was safe to go back. He didn't have to be part of Charles's plans.

"You're not going back," Charles whispered. "Bigger and better, my friend."

Sadly, bigger and better wouldn't be happily ever after. Not for anyone.

* * *

None of them knew how to fly a helicopter, but it didn't stop Charles from trying. He sat in the bloodied seat, after clearing the mess from the windshield, and played with the controls.

Rachel knew this was her chance. Morris refused to listen, but he'd see she was right once the deed was done. Just had to work up the courage.

"This is a terrible idea," George said. "What if you crash this thing?"

"We won't die, silly."

"We will if we go down in a ball of flames. Fairly sure a burning head results in brain death."

Rachel didn't say anything. She hoped Charles did kill them all. Then, at least, they wouldn't be part of his stupid plan. She didn't trust that whatever the parasite had done to them was a good thing, or permanent. They could die tomorrow or go insane, as Charles had. Or worse, they could become something that wasn't even human, and she would cease to exist. It'd just be the parasite controlling her soulless body.

The pressure of the gun burned against her back, as though urging her to just shoot him and be done with it. She wasn't sure why she didn't. There were several opportunities in the bunker. More as they followed Charles out of the facility to the helicopter. It had been dark, though, because Charles wanted to hide from the drones, so she couldn't be sure she wouldn't miss. Now, as he sat in front of her, head so close she couldn't miss, she had a chance she couldn't screw up.

But each time she thought about reaching for the gun, her hand remained in her lap.

"Ah," Charles said. "Maybe this button will do it."

The helicopter sputtered, but it didn't start. He tried again. Nothing.

"Hmm. Did you do something to it, Georgie?"

George sighed. "When would I have had the chance?"

"Good point. Perhaps we're out of fuel. Morris, would you and George please fetch the fuel truck so we can remedy the problem?"

Morris looked at Rachel. "Can't George do that by himself?"

"He could, if I trusted him."

"I won't run," George said. "Letting you loose in the world without supervision is worse than being your captive."

"Careful. It's almost sounding like you might be fond of me."

George snorted as he unbuckled his belt. "Come on, Morris. Let's get the gas so he can kill us all."

Morris didn't move.

"Oh, don't worry," Charles said. "Rachel is perfectly safe alone with me. She reminds me of my daughter, only prettier."

Rachel nodded. Morris looked at her hands and then his eyes shifted to where he knew she'd stashed the gun. "I'm fine," she said. "Go."

Morris and George got out of the helicopter. Charles was silent long enough for it to be uncomfortable. Finally, though, he spoke.

"Go on, love," he said. "You know you'll never be able to rest until you do what you think is right."

Rachel opened her mouth, but no words came out. He knew?

"Of course, I know. Don't be afraid. This is your only

chance. If you don't take it, you'll never get another."

"I'll do it," she said, taking the gun from her waistband. "Unless you stop this insanity and just let us go."

He chuckled. "Sorry, sweetheart, but I've been making plans for far too long to walk away. Do what you must, and I'll do what I must. I forgive you already, if that's what you're worried about."

She released the safety. The day before, after a lot of nagging from her, George had shown her how to make sure there was a round in the chamber. Warned her the gun would kick a little, so she should make sure she was really close, or adjusted her aim to account for the jerking of her wrist. He then told her the whole idea was crazy and insisted she toss the gun away.

"Okay," Charles said, without turning. "You're obviously nervous. Let's count down. Five seconds sound okay?"

"I'll do it."

"Maybe. Maybe not. If you don't do it now, I don't want to hear another word about it. Five... four... three..."

Rachel fired the gun.

* * *

Morris heard the shot as they neared the doors to the facility. Almost simultaneously, a fire erupted behind his eyes. He hit the ground as his knees buckled and heard George curse as he did the same. For several breathtaking seconds, he feared he might be dying. Wished for it a little. But suddenly, the pain stopped and he could hear birds chirping and George breathing heavily.

"What the fuck was that?" Morris asked.

George stood slowly. "She did it."

"What?"

"She killed him."

"We're screwed, aren't we?"

"Not if we play this right." George turned back toward

the helicopter. "We can manipulate thoughts."

Morris followed him. Rachel had exited the helicopter. Blood covered her face and hands. "According to Charles, we can."

"I don't think he lied about that."

"Tough to know if anything he said was truthful. It might have been him the whole time making us believe we have abilities we don't. He also said we were "infants" without the superior skills he's developed. Which do we believe?"

"I believe everything he said about the parasite and I know he's not lying about what we can do."

"I don't even know where to begin. How does one reach out to another mind? What do we say? Do we just think it? So many variables. We should practice first. Make sure it's possible."

"First, we don't have time to… practice. Jesus, Morris, I have trouble believing you're the genius Catherine described."

Morris frowned. He supposed he was overthinking. A little faith went a long way. "Fine," he said. "We can read thoughts and control people. How does that help us right now?"

"Because we can manipulate minds, we can make anything look the way we need it to look, right?"

"Sure?"

"So, I'll deal with my people. They won't know what I am now, and they'll think I saved the world from Charles and his schemes."

"And us?"

"You and Rachel will have to run."

"Why can't we go back to our—?"

"Charles would've ensured you can't. Not sure how, but he would've made it impossible for you to carry on as normal. I can only handle so many fires. Yours, I'm afraid, is not extinguishable."

"He's dead," Rachel said. She stumbled as she neared

them. "Did you guys feel it too?"

"What?" Morris asked.

"When he died. The headache."

He nodded. "Why'd you do that? We agreed you'd—"

"Why? Are you fucking serious, Mo?"

"Yes, I'm fucking serious. What did you think you'd accomplish?"

"We're free now. No world domination. No killing people."

"Which is great, but we still can't go home."

"Sure, we can."

George sighed. "You guys are making this harder than it needs to be. Go back to the facility. Second floor, room 209. Inside there's a safe. Combination is seventeen, twelve, two, twenty-nine. Open it, take whatever you can carry. There are passports, untraceable phones and cash inside. Take it all. The passports will require a photo, of course, but you can stick whatever on there and convince whoever's looking that it's real."

"Aren't you coming with us?" Morris asked.

"I can't," he pointed to the helicopter. "I have to run damage control. My people will come soon. I'll tell them Charles escaped, with your help. Sorry, but without knowing how he prepared for this, I have to sacrifice someone. I'll ensure no one finds you. I'll contact one of the phones if they're close, so you have a chance to run before they get too close. Christ, what a fucking mess."

"So, we just leave everything?" Morris asked. He couldn't live like that. All of his work. His patients...

"You have to. Now go. Get what you need. At the back of the facility is a parking garage. Take a staff vehicle. Don't take one with government plates. Do you know what those look like?"

"Yes," Rachel said.

"Good. They have GPS trackers, so if you took one of those, they'd find you in no time."

"Do you have keys to any of these cars?" Morris asked.

"No. Guess you don't know how to hot-wire one?"

He laughed. "Um, modern technology means hot-wiring isn't as easy as it used to be."

"Actually," George said, "Bill leaves his keys under the bumper. Right side, I think. Always losing them, he said. He drives—drove a red Honda. Two-door, I think. It'll be on the side of the lot closest to the building."

Morris still couldn't move. Couldn't believe this would be his life.

"Mo!" Rachel yelled. "Get your ass in gear. We have to go."

"No, there has to be a way to spin this so we can go back to our lives. We're not bad people. Charles made us do those things. George can tell them. Prove we're not a threat."

"They have footage of what you did at the hospital," George said. "Catherine's notes. My notes. We filed a police report and issued a warrant for Rachel's arrest too. She killed her own cousin."

"I didn't."

"You did, because Charles made you." George patted her shoulder. "Face it. There's no way out of this for the two of you."

"But my work..."

"Is over," Rachel said. "Come on. We'll get somewhere safe, and then, who knows? We could manipulate someone into giving you a job under a different name. You can still do your work. It'll just have to wait until the heat is off us."

"It'll never be off you guys," George warned. "You'll have to move frequently. Maybe just leave the country. Go somewhere without an extradition treaty."

"Shit," Morris said as it all sank in. "We're never going home."

"But Charles is dead and while the timing sucks, I'm glad Rachel killed him," George said. "It looks hopeless now but imagine if we'd done nothing and he was unleashed on the world. It would've been a bloodbath."

Morris knew he was right. Knew this was the only way. Still, he had hoped to change Charles's mind. To make him see the good they could do. Now...

"Go." George patted his back. "You've got less than an hour before someone shows up."

Morris let Rachel drag him back to the facility. She did what she had to. He understood that. Didn't stop the anger he felt. She just made the decision for everyone.

"I'm sorry, Mo," she said. "I know you hoped it would be different."

"We're all alone."

"No. We have each other. That's enough."

It'd have to be. For now.

CHAPTER 20

George managed to convince the team that arrived a little over an hour later that Charles escaped and the information they'd received was only half true. He confirmed Charles's claim, which was supported by video footage from the hospital and the facility, that Morris and Rachel helped Charles escape, but they took off when George killed Charles.

He let his superiors believe they were infected, and therefore vulnerable. No one knew what was missing from his safe, and he didn't plan to tell them. They questioned him for hours, but finally, he was allowed to clean himself up and get some sleep.

A day later, showered and properly rested, George sat in a small room across a metal table from his colleague, Todd Murphy. Just a debriefing, Todd claimed. To cross all the t's.

"So," Todd said. "The two suspects kidnapped you, while ill, and forced you to bring them here?"

"You already asked me this."

"Tell me again."

George sighed. He focused on Todd's eyes, willing him to believe his story so they could get back to normal. "They are infected, but they're well into the fourth stage, possibly the fifth, which means they're not completely incapacitated."

"How did they get out of quarantine?"

"Rachel was never in quarantine. We were unable to bring her in. She helped Morris escape by killing Dr. Fairchild. Charles was manipulating them from here."

"So, he does have the ability to influence minds over long distances."

"Did."

"Pardon?"

"He's dead. So, past tense."

"Right. Okay, so you were wrong about the extent of his abilities."

"Yes, and I think I paid a pretty high price for it. My career is in the shitter and my team is dead."

Todd smiled. "We are up against something way beyond the realm of known possibilities, and you eliminated the threat. Yes, people died, but your career is fine. Seriously, George, this is just to ensure the suits at the top are satisfied you weren't in on it. Anyone who knows you knows the truth."

God, he hoped not.

"So," Todd said. "Go on. What happened after Rachel released Morris from the hospital?"

"She didn't. I took him."

"You?"

"I was bringing him here, so he couldn't hurt anyone. I didn't realize that Charles was also guiding them here. He influenced the pilot and my men so Rachel could hide on the chopper. When we landed, the men were like infants waiting to be slaughtered. Just stood there while he murdered them."

"How did he kill them?"

"You saw the autopsies."

"I did. And you're saying he did all of that with his mind?"

George nodded. "I wouldn't have believed it if I hadn't seen it. You saw the video, so…"

"Tell me again, why we were keeping him alive?"

"Research. We hoped to be able to turn him. Use his abilities for our benefit."

Todd laughed. "Is someone who has turned, as you put it, really someone you can trust in the end?"

"I know. Terrible idea."

"And why didn't he kill you?"

"I was the only one who could open his cage."

Todd nodded. "Why did you open his cage?"

"My choices were open it or die."

"But he knew you were the only one who could open it, so your choices were actually open it, or refuse and leave the building so he couldn't hurt you."

"If I refused, and left the building, he'd have hurt a lot of people. Remember, I knew he could reach out to people outside of his prison, and he could control them. I figured, set him free, make him happy, and then, when he's not expecting it, eliminate the threat."

"He could've killed you once you set him free. From what I've heard, he could've done it without lifting a finger."

"I know. It was a calculated risk that paid off."

The light above them flickered. George knew Charles was dead. Saw his body. Checked his pulse himself. Still, that flickering, which used to happen often before they locked Charles in the cell, sent a chill over his skin.

"Okay," Todd said. "I guess enough is enough. I've asked you the same questions a million times, and your answer are pretty consistent. You're back in charge, sir, and I can finish these autopsies and go home."

"That's it?"

"That's it."

It was almost too easy. George stood with Todd. No point in looking a gift horse in the mouth. Charles was dead. Totally and truly. No coming back from a bullet in the brain.

Still…

"Hey," he said as Todd opened the door. "Could I take one last look at Charles's body before we cremate him?"

"Just making sure?" Todd asked and then laughed.

"Something like that."

"Sure. I think Mary's down there. She'll show you where they're keeping him. I doubt they'll be burning anything for a while. He's a medical mystery, so they'll be studying him until there's nothing left to sample."

"I figured as much. Thanks, Todd."

"No problem. Get some rest, okay? You look worse than dead."

He rubbed the stubble on his chin. "I'm good. Once I shave this mess, you won't even know I was the hostage of an alien parasite infected psychopath."

"Who was also your great grandfather." Todd winked.

"Let's forget that part. Forget all of it, actually."

"Forgotten."

"Thanks."

Todd blinked. "For what?"

The lights in the hallway flickered. George looked up and then back at Todd. Right, he had Charles's abilities. Didn't realize he could use them without trying. He smiled. "Just thanks. I'll talk to you later."

"Yeah, sure. Hey, want to grab a beer before I head back to Washington?"

"Sounds good. Give me a call when you're through. My schedule should be clear for a while."

* * *

The morgue, an outdated part of the facility that they hadn't used in years, smelled of alcohol and mold. George had followed Mary, a middle-aged woman with basic medical training and zero personal skills, to the basement without uttering much more than his name. She carried the conversation down the elevator, and then through the dimly lit hallways to the south section of the basement, an area George hadn't entered since his first week there.

"Brought those fancy doctors in yesterday," Mary was saying. "Instead of thanking me for tagging and preserving their bodies, I hear about how I fucked up. Ruined samples and bullshit like that."

"Did you take samples?" George asked.

"Fuck no," she turned, glared at him, and then faced forward again. "I put the poor bastards in bags and wrote their names on the tags, if I could identify them. Some, as you know, don't even got heads or faces. Then I just stuck 'em in the fridge. Like you all told me."

"You did well, Mary. Thanks."

"Tell those fuckers upstairs in the pretty coats. They think they own the goddamn world. I'd like to see them face real danger. Probably piss in their fancy pants if they saw real action."

"They would."

"Damn right," she sniffed. "Only reason I'm here is I'm the only one trained for both combat and medical. Ain't even a nurse. Just supposed to help out in the field, right?"

"And we appreciate it. Are we close yet?"

"Oh yeah," Mary turned right and then pointed to a door at the end of the hallway. "In there. Why'd they want him separated from the rest? He can't kill 'em any deader."

"He's infected with a parasite. We didn't want just anyone to handle his body. Could be contagious."

"Seriously?"

George nodded as she unlocked the door.

"Jesus. Good thing I never went in there. I was curious, mind you, but Murphy said leave him locked up, so I did."

"Good. I'd hate to see anything happen to you."

"So would I," she said and then laughed. The radio on her hip squawked. Mary sighed. "Those fucking nerds again. You okay for a few minutes?"

He didn't want to be alone, but the fear was silly, so he nodded. "I'll be fine."

"Door locks on its own when you leave. Just check to make sure. Never know, right?"

"Right."

Mary left without another word. George, holding the door open, stared inside the room. One gurney. A black bag on top. One light above. It was almost like someone staged it to look creepier than it already was.

George took a breath and then entered the room. He figured it'd smell of rotting flesh, but it didn't. It smelled like lemon and a hint of mold, which was probably growing in the cement walls. He approached the gurney slowly. So many years he'd viewed Charles as a permanent thing. Well, as long as George lived anyway. The plan had always been to try to reform him, make him a good guy, and if they couldn't, terminate him before George retired, because he couldn't be trusted with anyone else.

He never imagined it'd go like this. Charles killed by a girl barely out of high school, who would live forever in that pert young body. Unless someone took her head, which was possible. George wasn't entirely convinced that letting them go had been a good decision. He could hunt them down later, though, if the need arose. Terminate them himself without anyone questioning his actions.

Making them the villains definitely worked in his favor. Hell, so far, everything had worked in his favor, except his power and virtual immortality came at a cost; having those *things* living inside him. He pushed the thought aside. They were nothing. Just organic material rebuilding his body into something better. That's how he had to view it or he'd go insane.

"Good boy," Charles whispered.

George's skin tightened. He must be delusional. Tired, probably, still feeling the effects of the infection, definitely. Why, then, did the bag look like it was moving?

He could just leave. Should. Go and never look back.

"Where's the fun in that? Open the bag, Georgie."

The light above flickered. George's fingers twitched at his sides. How long did the hallucinations last? Maybe this whole nightmare was a delusion. He'd wake up at the university, Catherine would be at his bedside in one of those ugly white suits, praying for him to get better.

She'd smile when he opened his eyes, tell him they found a cure, and it'd all be like a bad dream. Charles would still be in his cell, the men and women who'd trained under him for most of their young careers would still be alive, waiting for him to return and take command once more.

"Open the bag," Charles said again.

George swallowed. His throat itched.

It wasn't real.

"Only one way to prove that," Charles said. "Come on, Georgie. You're not afraid, are you?"

No, he wasn't scared of a corpse. The thoughts in his head were another matter. Deep inside, a tiny part of him wished Charles weren't dead, because if he wasn't dead, George wasn't alone in this. It was a stupid wish. Charles would do immeasurable damage if he survived. That bag was the best place for him.

George heard a sigh and then the bag moved. He saw the zipper slide downward. A hand appeared. An arm, and then Charles sat up.

"No," George backed away from the gurney. "I saw you dead. Your head has a hole in it."

"And my skull was shattered right here," Charles pointed to the spot above his right ear, which showed no sign of trauma, aside from some dried blood.

"You're dead. I saw it. Made sure of it."

Charles smiled. "Yet here I am."

"How? Brain death kills—"

"A lie on my part. I apologize for deceiving you, Georgie, but I suspected you'd panic and kill me. Imagine my surprise when that sweet girl showed she had bigger balls than you."

"But we ran the tests. Explored every possibility. Brain death is brain death. There's no coming back from it."

"The parasite repairs the cells in my body, no matter what trauma you inflict upon it. I told you a bullet to the brain would kill me, because I needed you to believe you weren't entirely without options."

"Impossible. If that's true, all of those patients we—"

"They weren't fully evolved yet. A single parasite can't do the work on its own, not even a dozen can work quickly enough, so they are lost, sadly."

"I'm dreaming," George said. "You're dead. Everything is fine."

Charles sighed again. "Stop denying what's right in front of you. The only way to truly kill us is to sever our heads and make sure you separate the two parts. Otherwise, the organisms in our bodies will repair the tissue, make the necessary connections, and we will heal."

"I'll cut off your head then."

"That'd do it." Charles smiled. "Unless I'm lying again. This is fun."

George swallowed against the lump in his throat. "What do you want? I won't kill another innocent person."

"We've been over that," Charles extricated himself from the bag and hopped off the gurney. "Thank God they didn't take my clothes. That would've been awkward."

"You can't escape. This place is crawling with soldiers. They'll lock you up again. I won't have a choice but to let them."

"You always have a choice, Georgie. Right now, you have two: Help me leave this place or I will kill every soul in here, including you."

"I can't be killed. I'm like you."

Charles rolled his eyes. "You don't listen, do you? I said a severed head would do the trick. I wasn't lying. Sorry for messing with you. I understand why you would have some misgivings. We could try it and find out, if you need proof. Only, you'd be dead, so..."

George didn't want to be shackled to Charles for the rest of his life, especially if that life was now longer than expected, but he also didn't want to die. He could make a deal. Minimize the casualties by keeping Charles happy until... until what?

"Tick, tock, son," Charles said. "Someone's bound to come along any second, and your decision will be made for you. I'll spare their lives if you get with the program."

"What will you do after you leave?"

"Nothing. You need time to get stronger, as do I. While the bullet to my brain didn't kill me, it's taken an enormous amount of energy to heal. For now, we've got a campaign to plan, a couple of wayward children to track down, and then, I suppose I'll just wait for them."

"Who?"

Charles smiled. "Oh, I didn't tell you that part?"

"No, you didn't."

"Well," Charles said as he stretched. "I have a theory about the origins of our gift."

"It's alien. We've already proven that."

"Which means that somewhere out there, our benefactor is waiting to see what his or her... *its* seeds have produced."

"They would've returned by now if their plan were to invade. It's more likely they crashed, died, and whatever they were carrying, for whatever reason, was left behind, or the parasites are the aliens, and they've obviously got what they needed. There is no master plan. We were infected by something that was never meant to be here."

"Maybe they're already here." George didn't seem to hear him. "They could've been here all this time, waiting and watching."

"Unlikely."

"Look, they'd know of the crash and their precious cargo. Do you believe they'd just abandon what they've planted? With only a single flower in their garden? I don't think so. Now, we have four. They will come back."

"Rachel and Morris are gone. I told them to leave the country."

"They're never so far I can't reach them. Have a little faith." Charles pointed to the door. "Shall we?"

"They won't let you leave."

"You're so thick sometimes. They won't remember I was here, nor will they remember you, for that matter."

George closed his eyes. Willed reality to come back. Pleaded for it.

He heard a sigh.

"You got what you need?" Mary asked.

George opened his eyes. Charles's body laid on the gurney, although the zipper was open. He saw the smashed skull, the open, very dead eyes, and almost laughed. He imagined all of it. Christ, he was losing his mind.

"Takin' a nap there, sir?"

"What? Oh, no. Sorry. It's just I've spent so much time with him. Strange to imagine him gone."

"Yeah," she said. "You get used to it, though. Everyone's replaceable, right?"

George looked at her. Her brown eyes were kind if a little too wide, and her smile was genuine. Why did she make him feel so anxious, then?

"I'm off duty in ten," Mary said. "I'd like to get this all closed up, if you don't mind."

"Of course," George walked to the door. "I lost track of time. How long was I down here?"

"Half hour. I almost forgot about you."

As they exited, she said nothing. Her silence continued until George got on the elevator and pressed the button for the second floor. "You coming up?"

She shook her head. "I've got this soil sample from the university to take care of. Don't worry," she said as the door closed. "I'll be right behind you, *Georgie*."

CHAPTER 21

Rachel closed the trunk and then picked up the bags of groceries she set on the ground next to her car. As she walked toward the cottage, she inhaled the spring morning. Almost a year had passed since they left their lives. It was hard to believe they found something so... normal. A quiet cottage at the end of a private lane, on a lake so beautiful, it sometimes took her breath away to look at it. When they'd arrived in Toronto, George said it was too cramped. Too many people. Someone might recognize them. So, she'd followed him north, until they found this place. Mazinaw, the locals told them it was called. Morris put out feelers and found this cottage to rent. No one asked many questions. When they did, she and Morris gave vague answers. They didn't press for more details. She liked that.

They had no neighbors for a couple of miles. No one to whisper about Morris's strange morning walks where he mumbled to himself angrily or wonder at the objects that often floated in the sky. No one to care that wild animals, a lot of them, seemed drawn to their property. It still amazed her how a snarling coyote or a timid doe turned instantly docile and trusting, with a look or a word from her or Morris.

They had to know the limits of their abilities, Morris had said. It was important to understand and practice, should George ever turn them in. Her once trusting and docile professor suspected everyone of practically everything now. She missed the old Morris, but this one did have some appealing qualities. He took charge now, had a bit of an edge, and he actually noticed she existed.

True, he hadn't given in to the sexual tension between them, but time was on her side and his walls were crumbling. Just the other day he kissed her cheek before leaving for work at a gas station twenty miles away. He'd blushed and mumbled something she couldn't hear, but at least he'd done it, without any prompting from her.

It made her sad to see him don the grey shirt with the silly name tag every day. As he fastened the buttons, his shoulders slumped just a little, and his smile disappeared. Morris's fate was so much more than that. He could've lived anywhere, done anything. Could've persuaded a hospital to hire him, even though he had no credentials, or a university to take him on as a professor. He chose to lay low, he'd said. Working as a doctor or a researcher meant papers. Publication. He'd be recognized.

Maybe in a couple of years, she could talk him around to going back to what he loved.

She opened the door and entered the cottage. Once again, Morris had closed the blinds, plunging the happy little living room into darkness.

"You napping again?" she asked, setting the bags on the coffee table.

Morris looked up. "No." He waved the remote in his hand. "News."

"Anything interesting?"

"Something about an infection," he said. "Causes migraines. First cases were in Washington, and it's spread to New York and Boston."

"Strange pattern."

"If there's a single vector, it's not. The pattern of infection would follow the travel pattern of the source."

"You don't think…"

He shrugged. "If it is, we'll be fine."

"So, we're not going to—?"

"No."

The news anchor flashed his perfect white teeth, said something about exciting news in Washington and then turned the mic over to his colleague. The White House appeared; a man stood on the lawn in front of a crowd. The camera zoomed in.

Rachel's breath caught in her chest. "When was this?"

"Yesterday," Morris said.

The camera angle changed. They saw the side of a familiar

face. Rachel bit her lip.

"Jesus Christ," Morris whispered. "Do you see this?"

She sat on the armrest. "Wish I could say no, but I see it."

There, on the small, dusty screen, was George. Smiling widely, he shook hands with various people as he made his way down the steps, toward a throng of reporters. Beneath the video, a subtitle repeated over and over again.

"President George Danvers holds first press conference at the White House..."

As the video followed George through the crowd, Rachel felt Morris's hand on hers. She threaded her fingers through his. Every person in the crowd stared at George adoringly, as though he might be the Messiah. Rachel swallowed the bile that stung her throat.

George, clapping an elderly man on the back, waved a final time before the angle changed, showing a black car waiting for him. A man stood next to the car, also grinning widely.

"Is that...?" she couldn't finish.

"Can't be."

Rachel blinked as the news program went to commercial. "We're overreacting. Probably just seeing things because we're upset."

Morris nodded. "I mean, we saw what we saw. No question about what happened. Right?"

A car door closed outside.

Rachel's heart skipped. "Just the neighbors."

"We don't have any."

"Right. A... someone's lost?"

Morris walked to the window behind the television. He lifted the slats of the blind. "Shit."

A knock on the door. Morris didn't move. Rachel took a step, but he shook his head and put a finger to his lips.

"I know you're in there," Charles said. "But if you'd like to play the game, I suppose it won't hurt. Don't be afraid. I come in peace."

"Smug prick," Morris grumbled.

Rachel walked to the door. It was solid wood, except for a

small pane of glass at the top. She stood next to the glass and quickly peered outside. Charles stood a few feet from the door. He smiled and lifted a sword.

"Oh God," she whispered. "Why is he carrying a sword?"

"To kill us."

"You have two choices," Charles said. "Be smart and come back to me, where you belong," he looked at the sword, "or die."

Morris made a noise in his throat. It sounded like a sob. "He won't. Can't. We're valuable to him."

"What do we do?" Rachel asked. "I won't be like George. We promised we wouldn't be his puppets, no matter what happened."

"I was afraid it might come to this." Morris walked slowly to the cabinet beside the sofa. He opened the drawer, shoulders slumped. He just stood there, staring at whatever was inside.

"I'll count to ten," Charles called. "How's that? One... two..."

"Mo?"

Morris turned around. He raised his arm. "We've got one choice, Rachel. You know it."

She closed her eyes. "Do it."

* * *

George stayed in the car until he heard the gunshot. Birds exploded from a nearby tree. Charles stood, sword still held in the air, near the front door of the rundown cottage. He didn't move as George exited the vehicle. A second shot echoed in the stillness of the morning. Charles said nothing as George touched his arm, forcing him to lower the sword.

"I guess you have their answer," George said. "They'd rather die."

Charles nodded. "I'm sure they'll change their minds in the morning. Come on. Let's get them in the car before some hiker investigates those shots."

"Why not just leave them? We don't need their help."

"They're family, Georgie. We don't abandon family."

"No, they're—"

"We share DNA now. That makes us all blood. I walked out on my family once. It won't happen again."

"But if they'd rather die, then who are we to say they can't?"

"We're *gods*, Georgie."

Charles walked up the steps. He swung the sword almost joyfully as he whistled.

About the Author

Renee Miller lives in Tweed, Ontario. She writes in multiple genres, but prefers dark fiction with strong elements of horror, erotica and/or comedy.

She is the author of several novels and novellas, most recently *Retail*, *Church* and *She Ain't Pretty* from Unnerving Press.

ALSO FROM BLOODSHOT BOOKS

JANUARY 12, 1888

When a day dawns warm and mild in the middle of a long cold winter, it's greeted as a blessing, a reprieve. A chance for those who've been cooped up indoors to get out, do chores, run errands, send the children to school... little knowing that they're only seeing the calm before the storm.

The blizzard hits out of nowhere, screaming across the Great Plains like a runaway train. It brings slicing winds, blinding snow, plummeting temperatures. Livestock will be found frozen in the fields, their heads encased in blocks of ice formed from their own steaming breath. Frostbite and hypothermia wait for anyone caught without shelter.

For the hardy settlers of Far Enough, in the Montana Territory, it's about to get worse. Something else has arrived with the blizzard. Something sleek and savage and hungry. Wild animal or vengeful spirit from native legend, it blends into the snow and bites with sharper teeth than the wind.

It is called the *wanageeska*.
It is the WHITE DEATH

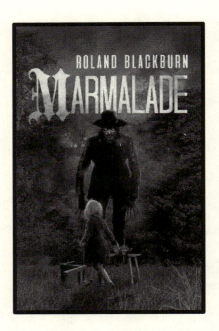

IF SHE SAYS HIS NAME, HE WILL COME

The lone witness to her father's grisly murder, recently orphaned Prose Harden finds herself locked away at Everbrook, a group home for emotionally disturbed teenagers, until the police can find enough evidence to charge her. But she knows who killed her father.

SHE'S KNOWN HIM ALL HER LIFE

They always thought he was imaginary, even when the bodies piled up. But whenever the Marmalade Man arrives, blood follows. As Prose struggles to escape, she discovers that something hungry lurks behind the institution's walls, she knows her old friend is drawing ever closer. With nothing left to lose, Prose strikes a bargain with the county psychiatrist: an early release if she explains the death of her mother, the disappearance of her stepmother, and what actually happened in that deserted cabin one week ago.
Can Prose be freed before her dark savior reaches her side, or will what hides behind the walls of Everbrook consume her?

ALL SHE HAS TO DO IS SAY HIS NAME

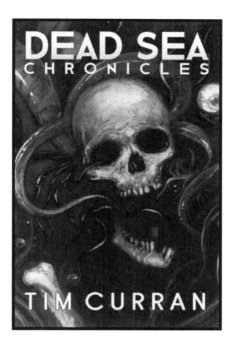

RETURN TO THE DEAD SEA

Come back to a mist-shrouded realm of horrors outside our own world...

Come back to a place where rotting hulks drift on brackish tides and the nightmares of wayward travelers come to hideous life...

Come back to a rancid ocean choked with a tangled maze of moldering vegetation and the decomposing carcasses of those who died screaming for rescue...

Come back to a world where predators soar through noxious clouds, aquatic leviathans lurk in the currents below and the souls of lost sailors suffer an infinite torment on their final voyages...

DEAD MEN MAY TELL NO TALES...
BUT THE DEAD SEA DOES.

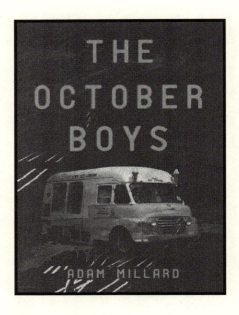

HALLOWEEN, 1988

A gang of twelve-year-old boys are trick-or-treating in London. Off in the distance, they hear the discordant chimes of an ice-cream truck. It seems strange to hear on a cold autumnal night, but their thoughts of maximizing their candy haul soon dismissed its incongruous melody... until they saw the rusting hulk idling in the shadows at the end of the street, its driver a faceless shadow.

That was the night he took one of them.

OCTOBER, 2016

Years later, Halloween is fast approaching and Tom Craven is still haunted by the events of that dark night, especially the fact that their friend was never found. Increasingly plagued by horrific visions, Tom returns to the place where it all began, only to discover he's not the only one who can feel it. His friends have already arrived and are preparing for a battle which could get them all killed.

The Ice Cream Man is back... *and he's come for the ones that got away.*

From a crater lake on an island off the coast of Bronze Age Estonia...

To a crippled Viking warrior's conquest of England ...

To the bloody temple of an Aztec god of death and resurrection...

Their presence has shaped our world. They are the Riders.

One month ago, an urban explorer was drawn to an abandoned asylum in the mountains of northern Massachusetts. There he discovered a large specimen jar, containing something organic, unnatural and possibly alive.

Now, he and a group of unsuspecting individuals have discovered one of history's most horrific secrets. Whether they want to or not, they are caught in the middle of a millennia-old war and the latest battle is about to begin.

There's a monster coming to the small town of Pikeburn. In half an hour, it will begin feeding on the citizens, but no one will call the authorities for help. They are the ones who sent it to Pikeburn. They are the ones who are broadcasting the massacre live to the world. Every year, Red Diamond unleashes a new creation in a different town as a display of savage terror that is part warning and part celebration. Only no one is celebrating in Pikeburn now. No one feels honored or patriotic. They feel like prey.

Local Sheriff Yan Corban refuses to succumb to the fear, paranoia, and violence that suddenly grips his town. Stepping forward to battle this year's lab-grown monster, Sheriff Corban must organize a defense against the impossible. His allies include an old art teacher, a shell-shocked mechanic, a hateful millionaire, a fearless sharpshooter, a local meth kingpin, and a monster groupie. Old grudges, distrust, and terror will be the monster's allies in a game of wits and savagery, ambushes and treachery. As the conflict escalates and the bodies pile up, it becomes clear this creature is unlike anything Red Diamond has unleashed before.

No mercy will be asked for or given in this battle of man vs monster. It's time to run, hide, or fight. It's time for Red Diamond.

ON THE HORIZON FROM BLOODSHOT BOOKS

2022

The Obese – Jarred Martin
Pound of Flesh – D. Alexander Ward
Popsicle – Christa Wojciechowski
Schafer – Timothy G. Huguenin
The Amazing Alligator Girl – Kristin Dearborn
Fairlight – Adrian Chamberlin
Ungeheuer – Scott A. Johnson
Teach Them How to Bleed – L.L. Soares

Someday. I Promise

Blood Mother: A Novel of Terror – Pete Kahle
The Abominations (The Riders Saga #2) – Pete Kahle
The Horsemen (The Riders Saga #3) – Pete Kahle

* AND BEYOND

BLOODSHOT BOOKS

READ UNTIL YOU BLEED

Made in United States
Troutdale, OR
01/25/2024

17152156R10135